Love Lessons

Heavenly Bites Novella #2

◆

Christine S. Feldman

Printed by CreateSpace

Love Lessons first published via Kindle Direct © 2013 by Christine S. Feldman

ISBN-13: 978-1544943107

ISBN-10: 1544943105

Cover Design by - Elaina Lee

Cover Images - © Fotolia

For everyone celebrating a fresh start—and maybe a new year

CHRISTINE S. FELDMAN

CONTENTS

ACKNOWLEDGMENTS

This one is definitely for my family...
Thank you!

❖ Chapter One ❖

"DEAR, COULD I POSSIBLY get you to do something for me?"

On the surface, the question seemed harmless enough, especially when the petite white-haired lady asking it looked like she could have stepped right out of a Norman Rockwell painting. When one actually knew the matchmaking schemer that lay beneath that innocent exterior, though, one learned to pay close attention before committing to anything.

And Nadia Normandy had long ago learned to pay *very* close attention. Straightening from behind the Heavenly Bites display case in which she was rearranging a tray of cream puffs, she put both hands squarely on the counter and leaned forward to look the older woman straight in the eye. Well, forward

1

and down; Mrs. Beasley was only four foot eleven. "Who is he, Mrs. B?"

Her customer blinked at her through enormous tortoiseshell glasses, her eyes wide with innocence. Considering how much the huge lenses magnified her eyes, they looked very wide indeed. "I'm sure I don't know what you mean."

"Last time you asked me to do something for you with that little quaver in your voice, I wound up agreeing to a blind date with a carpet salesman who had an absolutely out-of-this-world sweating problem. What was wrong with that poor man anyway? Was it something glandular?"

"My dry cleaner's son is very nice," Mrs. Beasley huffed with what struck Nadia as incredibly insincere indignation.

"He used my cashmere scarf to wipe his forehead at dinner. Twice."

"Yes, but he did offer to get it cleaned for you at his mother's shop for a fantastic discount."

"Sorry, Mrs. B." Nadia bent down to resume working on the cream puffs. "I can find my own dates just fine, thank you." She'd gotten nibbles from three different prospects this week alone due to all the holiday parties she'd attended. A hunky physical trainer, a Latin musician with a smile to die for, and the third one—what was he again? A dogwalker? Dog trainer maybe? Or maybe he just liked dogs. All she really remembered about him was his great tan because she was impressed that he managed to maintain it so well despite it being the middle of winter. Well, maybe she was more curious than impressed.

The fact that his tan was the only memorable thing about him was a bad sign, though. She'd give him the benefit of the doubt and one date, but somehow she suspected there wouldn't be a second one.

"Pretty thing like you? Of course you don't need help finding somebody." And yet it was impossible to miss the glance Mrs. Beasley gave to the ringless finger on Nadia's left hand, especially since her eyes were magnified to twice their normal size by her tremendous lenses.

Nadia raised one eyebrow to let her know that she understood exactly what that look meant but chose not to comment.

"And anyway," the older woman continued, "that wasn't the kind of favor I was going to ask of you."

"No?"

"No."

Closing up the display case, Nadia returned her attention to Mrs. Beasley. "So there's no man involved in this favor whatsoever?"

"Well…"

Now Nadia raised both eyebrows. "Uh huh, that's what I thought."

"It is *not* what you think. You see, the young man who handles all of my financial matters for me is a sweet boy, but he's also rather…awkward."

"Awkward?"

"Socially speaking, yes. You see, Benji—"

"Benji? This guy is named after a dog? *And* he's an accountant—oh, Mrs. B…" Shaking her head, Nadia reached for a cloth and began wiping down the counter.

"Benji is short for Benjamin actually, but Benji really suits him better. You'll see what I mean when you meet him."

"Mrs. B, I am not going out with your accountant."

"I'm not asking you to see him socially, dear, I'm asking you to…to *educate* him."

Nadia blinked and stopped wiping the counter. "Educate him? In what, scones and shortbread?"

"In social niceties, particularly in regards to women. How to talk to them, where to meet them, that sort of thing." Mrs. Beasley patted Nadia on the hand. "You're so good with people, dear. You'd be a natural at this!"

"At teaching a man how to pick up women? Mrs. B, what exactly do you think I do when I go out?"

"Who better to teach a man what women want than a woman?"

It was hard to argue with that. Still, the prospect of becoming a dating coach to a complete stranger was about as appealing as a second date with the uber-moist carpet salesman. "What about asking your granddaughter? She's not exactly shy with other people. Why not have her do it?"

Mrs. Beasley fidgeted and cleared her throat. "Aimee is… unconventional. I'm not sure she'd be the best person to give Benji advice on dating."

Unconventional. That was a good word for Aimee. The girl was probably a few years younger than Nadia, somewhere in her mid-twenties, and she had come to live with her grandmother a few months ago. In that short time, she'd gone from blonde to redhead to jet-black hair with red streaks. Nadia tried to picture Aimee even in the same room as an accountant and failed. "Fair enough."

"Then you'll do it?"

Nadia couldn't hold back a wince. "Mrs. B—"

"Please, dear? It's for a good cause, I promise."

"Is this because Trish is dating Ian now, and you want a matchmaking project?" Nadia asked, referring to her best friend and business partner. "Who's next on your list, your pharmacist?"

"No," Mrs. Beasley replied without a moment's hesitation. "My hairdresser."

Nadia started to laugh and then stopped as she realized the other woman was serious. "Wait—you actually do have a list?"

"Never mind that, dear. Now, Benji works nine to five most days, so it would probably be best if you met him after work."

"Hang on, I never said I'd—"

"Please, dear? At my age, I have so few pleasures left, and who knows how much time I even have at all, really." The quaver was back in Mrs. Beasley's voice, and she let one wrinkled hand hover tremulously over her heart as if it might give out on her within the next three seconds.

It was blatant manipulation, Nadia thought. It was also very effective. "Mrs. B," she groaned, pleading.

"You could consider it a Christmas present to me."

"I gave you your favorite homemade lemon tarts as your Christmas present!"

The old woman let both hands tremble over her heart now.

"Shame on you," Nadia muttered, folding her arms across her chest and frowning but also slumping against the back counter in defeat.

Mrs. Beasley beamed at her. "I think the best thing would be for you two to meet at that charming little coffee shop on Third and Oakdale," she told Nadia, the quaver in her voice vanishing as quickly as it had appeared. "It's midway between both of your workplaces." Reaching into her purse with a hand that was as steady as a rock, she pulled out a business card that had MacGready Financial Services, Inc. printed on it and handed it to Nadia. "I wrote the address on the back along with Benji's phone number. I'll tell him to expect you."

"What? Mrs. B, it's Christmas Eve!"

"You're right," Mrs. Beasley agreed after a moment's consideration. "Silly me. I suppose the day after Christmas is more reasonable."

"The day after Christmas—" Nadia sputtered, incredulous.

The older woman's lip quivered. "I just thought it would be so nice to help Benji start the new year off right, and—and—" Her hand found its way to her heart again.

Clearly Mrs. B meant to have her way in this. "All right, fine, Mrs. B. I'll do it. But you know, woman, you really ought to be regulated by the federal government. I'll bet you can squeeze out tears on command, can't you?"

Mrs. Beasley only patted Nadia's hand again. "How does five o'clock sound?"

"Like emotional blackmail, but other than that, fine."

"Lovely. Then I'll just take a dozen of those gingerbread men, and I'll be on my way."

Scooping up the requested treats and putting them in a bag, Nadia rang them up and handed them over. "I don't even have the first idea of what to say to this guy, you know."

"You'll think of something wonderful, dear, I just know it."

"Mrs. B?"

The woman paused with her hand on the door. "Yes?"

"Am I on that list of yours?"

"Merry Christmas, dear," was all Mrs. Beasley called out in response as she stepped out into the wintry weather.

Nadia stared after her. "Girl," she said aloud to herself in the empty bakery, "I have the distinct feeling that you are in deep trouble."

◆ ◆ ◆

"A DATING COACH, HUH?" Trish said to her later that evening over the sounds of blaring holiday tunes as the two of them sampled punch at the Christmas Eve party of a mutual friend. "How did she manage to talk you into that?"

"With a guilt trip that would have made any mama proud to call it her own."

"Well, maybe it won't be as bad as you think," Trish suggested. "You might even enjoy it. Come on, you give me advice on my love life all the time. Whether I ask for it or not."

"Excuse me, but if I had not given you and your love life a little nudge, would you be here tonight with a certain easy-on-the-eyes landscape architect?"

"No," Trish conceded, a goofy smile spreading across her face as her eyes found Ian on the other side of the room chatting with another guest. She even blushed.

No was right, Nadia thought, seeing the blush and grinning with a certain smug satisfaction. Sure, she had strong opinions and a habit of offering unsolicited advice. So? She was good at it. And frankly, some people really needed it. Badly. "I rest my case."

"See, though? That's what I'm saying. You might even have fun taking this guy under your wing."

A socially-awkward accountant? Oh, yes, oodles of fun, she thought. "I prefer to spend my time with men who already know what women like, thank you."

"You do, huh?"

"Yes."

Trish nodded her head toward Nadia's date, a tall and perfectly groomed dreamboat of a man who was in town for the week from Argentina to show one of his art exhibits at local museums. He'd hit on Nadia in the midst of his own show, which had been very flattering. At the moment he was talking to a rapt audience of half a dozen women who all seemed to take turns batting their eyelashes at him. "So does that describe Marcos there pretty well?"

"Matías," Nadia corrected her, sipping her punch.

"Sorry, Matías. So does he fit the bill?"

Nadia watched him gesture heavenward with a burst of energy as he spoke, his eyes wide as he waxed on about whatever his topic was. Color and light, maybe. Or texture. He'd talked for nearly an hour at dinner about texture, though, so surely he had exhausted that particular subject. The spark of interest he'd inspired in her after their first encounter had rapidly dwindled. "He's an amazingly talented artist. The things that man can do with paint—"

"That wasn't quite what I asked you."

No, she supposed it wasn't. "He's very charming."

Trish gave her a look. "But…?"

"'But' nothing. We had a couple of dates, it was nice, and tomorrow he flies back to Argentina. End of story."

"Oh. Sorry," Trish offered, a sympathetic look on her face.

"I'm not. We had fun. Honest, it's fine," Nadia told her, amused. "Don't look at me like my dog died." She noticed then the look that Ian cast in Trish's direction, and she nudged her friend, happy to change the subject. "Hey, I think your honey wants to dance with you, Trish. Or possibly devour you, judging by the way he's looking at you. Go over there and put him out of his misery, would you?"

"If I have to, I have to," Trish returned, but her adolescent grin was back. So was her blush.

"Girlfriend, he's got you acting like a teenager all over again, you know."

"Yep. Hold this, would you?"

Funny, Nadia thought as she accepted her friend's punch cup, but for someone as worldly as she was, she wouldn't mind feeling like a teenager again.

Just for a little while.

❖ Chapter Two ❖

CHRISTMAS DAY ITSELF WAS a bit of a blur to Nadia. Morning at her mother's house where family members who hadn't seen each other since last Christmas all gathered, a phone call to her father to wish him happy holidays—she'd had to wait until she'd left her mother's for that one, knowing the mere mention of her father's name would likely cause a very un-Christmas-like reaction—and then on to not one but two different parties at the homes of friends. A final round of Christmas caroling with a handful of friends along snowy streets had capped off the day.

Then it was back home to collapse on the couch with the uncomfortable feeling that she had drunk way too much eggnog that day and would likely pay for it later. Shoes off and feet up on the coffee table, she'd fallen asleep in that position with her last waking thought being to wonder how on earth another year had passed so rapidly.

And now it was December twenty-sixth, and after a day spent baking and hobnobbing with customers, Nadia found herself running late to meet Mrs. Beasley's young accountant at the proposed coffee shop.

Wondering for the umpteenth time how she had allowed Mrs. B to talk her into this, Nadia spotted the shop up ahead and lengthened her stride, blinking her eyes against a flurry of powdery snowflakes. Five minutes. Ten at most. She could fill ten minutes of time, surely. If this guy was as clueless about women as Mrs. B had led her to believe, she could throw him the basics and call it good. And then she could go home and put her aching feet up.

Be a good listener. Look a woman in the eye when she's talking. Don't wipe your forehead on any of her accessories...

Stepping into the coffee shop and brushing a dusting of snow off her shoulders, Nadia glanced around at the people already inside.

A couple with their heads close together at a cozy table for two, giggling the way new lovers always seemed to do...

A silver-haired man in a denim jacket sipping his coffee with an almost grim determination...

A trio of middle-aged ladies talking in low tones...

And a guy in a suit with a briefcase beside his feet and an overcoat draped on the arm of his chair. His back was to her, allowing her to see how the ends of his short, dark hair were trimmed so evenly along his neck that she could have used his hairline as a straightedge.

Yep. Accountant, she thought.

The sooner she got this over with, the sooner she could go home and soak in the tub. Weaving around a few other tables that were in her way, Nadia stopped in front of the man, plastering a smile onto her face. "Twenty bucks says you're Benji."

Startled, the young man looked up at her. Behind wire-rimmed glasses, his remarkably bright blue eyes blinked at her, and she could have sworn he did a double take at the sight of her. "Benjamin Garner, yes." He stood quickly and held out his hand.

"Miss Normandy?"

"Please. Call me Nadia, honey." Firm handshake, she thought, pleasantly surprised. That was a good sign. "Sorry I'm late," she added, removing her coat and laying it over the back of the chair that was opposite him. "Bakery got slammed five minutes before my shift was supposed to end." It actually might be time to consider hiring some extra help, which was kind of exciting. Business was going well.

"Not a problem."

"Hang on, I'm going to grab an espresso, okay? Be right back." He nodded, and she left him to go give her drink order at the counter. While she waited for the barista to prepare it, Nadia turned and took advantage of the opportunity to study Mrs. B's accountant.

He definitely looked like a stereotypical number cruncher with the crisp suit and tie and the way not a single hair on his head looked out of place, but although he was certainly no linebacker, his shoulders were broader than she expected. The suit was ample enough to make it impossible for her to tell just how well he did or did not fill it out, but she guessed he was on the lean side. Tall, too. Tall was good.

Mr. Garner—no, that wouldn't work, Nadia thought. He was too young for her to call him mister, possibly even a year or two younger than her. It would have to be Benji—Benji glanced up then and caught her staring at him, and then he began fidgeting self-consciously with his tie.

Nadia, on the other hand, was not the least bit embarrassed to have been caught staring. If she was supposed to help this guy out, after all, she had to appraise the situation fully, and her appraisal was…

He was cute, she decided finally as she took the espresso that the girl behind the counter handed to her. Not pretty-boy cute, although he did have pleasing features, but an awkward sort of cute that could actually work quite well for him if someone was to teach him how to use it to his advantage. Enter one Nadia Normandy.

Benji stood again as she returned to the table and then waited until she was seated before he sat down.

Good manners, too, she observed. *Somebody's mama raised him right.* All in all, things looked more promising than she'd anticipated.

"So, Miss Normandy—"

"You've got beautiful eyes," she told him suddenly, peering into them. And he really did, even hidden behind those wire frames. "That's going to work in your favor. Remember that."

"Oh." He blinked at her as if startled by her words and then turned faintly pink. "Okay. Thank you."

She nestled back in her chair, which, she was regretfully aware, was not nearly as comfortable as a tubful of bubbles and hot water. "So, I assume you've got some questions for me. Or do you want me to just dive right in?"

He shook himself out of his apparent daze. "I have a few questions, of course, but it might be better to start with a general overview of your expectations."

"*My* expectations?" His remark struck her as odd, but maybe he was merely trying to be an accommodating pupil. Nadia took a sip of her espresso and then leaned forward, lowering her voice in a conspiratorial way. "You know…"

Benji leaned in to listen.

"…I should probably tell you that when Mrs. B suggested this to me, I thought she was off her rocker. I'm not exactly an expert in these kinds of things, but you seem like a nice enough guy, so I'm going to do my best, all right?"

He squinted as if having trouble following her. "I—all right."

She leaned back again. "But I'll be honest, honey. My feet are killing me, and all I really want to do is go home and soak in a hot bath, so maybe we could do the Cliffs Notes version here, okay?"

"I'd be happy to schedule an appointment for you during my normal business hours, if you'd prefer, so we could take our time."

Was it her imagination, or did he emphasize the word normal as if she was intruding on *his* time? "An appointment?" Nadia shook her head and tried not to let her flicker of irritation show. He'd most likely been strong-armed into doing this as well, but still, how exactly did he think any of this was benefiting *her*? "Look, I'm not sure what Mrs. B told you, but I understood this to be a one-time kind of thing. No offense, it's just—my schedule's a little on the full side."

"I understand," he said, frowning slightly. "So is mine. But in order to really give your financial goals the attention they deserve, I don't recommend we rush through anything, Miss Normandy."

"Nadia."

"Nadia," he agreed.

His words sank in then, and Nadia abruptly straightened. "Wait a minute—what did you say?"

"I'm just trying to point out that financial planning isn't something you want to just pay lip service to. It—"

"Financial planning?" she repeated, her eyes widening as an ominous suspicion took root. "You think I'm here to talk about my *finances*?"

"Well, the short answer would be 'yes,'" Benji said, a wary expression on his face. "Did I misunderstand something? Why are you here then?"

"Because I'm a little old lady's pawn, apparently."

"Huh?"

Nadia sighed. *Mrs. B, I love you, but I'm going to kill you.* "What exactly did Mrs. B say to you to get you to come here today?"

Benji rubbed his forehead as if it ached. "She asked me to do her a favor, and she said something about this friend of hers. You," he added, gesturing at her.

"Yeah, but what was the something?"

"You know, come to think of it, she was kind of vague," he admitted, and then he frowned. "I don't think she actually came right out and said financial planning, it was just somehow implied. How did she do that?"

"Because she's very gifted at that sort of thing," Nadia told him grimly. "I hate to be the one to break it to you, but you got set up, and you got set up *good*."

"Set up how? What did—wait. Is this…is this a date?"

"No."

"Oh."

She thought he sounded a little disappointed, and it was impossible not to be flattered by that. "Consider me as more of a coach."

"In what?"

"In women."

Benji made a sort of choking sound, and his blush returned.

Feeling a flicker of sympathy—and perhaps a tiny bit of satisfaction after his earlier impatience with her—Nadia patted his hand. "Do you need a minute?"

"No," he sputtered. "But a graceful exit would be nice." His answer made Nadia grin, and he noticed. "What?"

That awkward sort of cuteness he possessed was showing through again, and it was beginning to grow on her. "Nothing, it's just—I think I know why Mrs. B chose you as her next project."

"Because I'm gullible?"

"You've got a certain something buried underneath that suit and tie. You're a nice guy, you're funny, you're cute…you've got definite potential. You just need somebody to help you bring it out, that's all." Nadia gestured at his suit, well-pressed and wrinkle-free. "Plus you've got this whole neat and tidy thing going on that could actually work to your advantage. There's something about a guy who's all prim and proper."

He raised his eyebrows, reeking of skepticism. "There is?"

"Yeah." A slow smile spread across Nadia's face. "It just kind of makes a woman want to mess him all up."

This time the blush even spread to his ears.

Oh, this was fun. She'd never met a man who turned red so easily before. Hopefully the fact that she found herself enjoying it didn't mean she was some kind of sadist, but the truth was that Benji here was starting to intrigue her. When was the last time that happened with a man?

She couldn't remember.

"You know what? Screw it," Nadia said abruptly, picking up her espresso and leaning back in her chair again. "I'm in."

"In what?"

"This," she returned, gesturing at the two of them and feeling a flicker of unexpected anticipation.

"Whatever it is. Yes, Mrs. B manipulated us both into it, and I'm *so* going to have a chat with her about that later, but I'm in. You want to learn about women? I'm going to help you. By the time I'm done with you, women are going to be tripping over themselves to get to you."

"I don't think—"

"Sorry, honey, but Mrs. B's already got you in her sights, so there's really not much point in trying to fight it. If I walk away now, she'll just find some other way to get you out on the meat market. You do realize that, don't you?"

Benji stared at her for a long moment and then slowly slumped back against his chair as if stunned.

Oh, yes, he was adorable.

Nadia grinned at him over her coffee cup. "Don't worry. I'll be gentle."

◆ ◆ ◆

"IT WAS A SCAM?" Trish asked her the next morning as they hustled to get batches of freshly baked scones out of the ovens before they got overly brown.

Nadia handed her an oven mitt. "Are you really all that surprised?"

"Not really, I guess. Think she'll show her face in here today, or do you think she'll be too embarrassed?"

"Ha! Mrs. B? Are you kidding? She'll probably pop in and demand to know what kind of progress I'm making and whether or not Benji's engaged to a nice girl yet."

"Benji." Trish rolled the name around on her tongue a few times and shook her head.

"She was right, though. It really does suit him."

"So you're really going to tutor him, huh?"

Setting out scones to cool, Nadia nodded. "First lesson is today. I made him promise to meet me for lunch before he had time to think about it. You know, I'm starting to think this whole thing could be kind of fun. I mean, I've never had official carte blanche to make over a man before."

"Carte blanche, eh? Did he really say that?"

Actually, he hadn't said much of anything after she asked him to meet for lunch—well, okay, maybe it was more like *informed* him where and when they would meet—and she'd left him sitting in the coffee shop with a rather dazed look on his face. But she had chosen to interpret his lack of a "no" as permission to go ahead. "Not in those words," she hedged.

"Really?" Trish looked at her suspiciously. "Which words did he use then?"

"Oh, come on," Nadia returned, dodging the question ever so slightly and fully aware that she was doing it. "If I don't help the guy out, who knows what Mrs. B will try next with him. He's better off in my capable hands, trust me. A week with me, and he'll be a changed man."

"Cocky much?"

"Hey, I just know what people need, and I'm good at what I do."

Trish's eyes widened with mock innocence. "Oh, you mean bossing other people around?"

"Careful," Nadia warned her, picking up a scone. "I have excellent aim."

"All right, all right…"

Nadia put the scone down and resumed removing the rest from the tray. "I'll take very good care of Benji."

"You're so selfless and giving."

"Sarcasm might be risky, Trish."

"No, I mean it. You're incredibly caring and generous. Especially with your friends."

"Well, thank you, girlfriend. I—" Suddenly Nadia realized Trish was looking at her hopefully. She grew wary. "Wait a minute, what are you—"

"In fact, I'll bet you'd just love to help your good buddy Trish out tonight and babysit Kelsey so that Ian and I could go to the movies and have a little alone time, wouldn't you?" Trish said, the words coming out in a rush as if she hoped the sheer speed of them would overwhelm Nadia into agreeing.

"Babysitting?" Nadia winced, dismayed. "Trish—"

"I'll be your best friend."

"You already are my best friend."

"I'll be your best friend even more," Trish offered, pleading. "Kelsey's a great kid. You'll love her, I swear."

"Mmm," Nadia said in return. She paused in removing scones to look at her friend more closely. "You're really falling hard for this guy, aren't you?"

"Little bit, yeah."

Again, Nadia felt that flicker of wistfulness, but she buried it. "Lucky for you, I'm a romantic at heart."

"Is that a yes?"

"Far be it from me to deprive you of time with your honey." Nadia pointed a finger at her. "But I am not, under any circumstances, watching cartoons. Deal?"

"Deal." Trish clasped her hands together in delight and beamed at her. "Yay! Thank you. We'll even bring you candy from the concession stand, if you like."

"Candy, wow. My night is looking up."

"Well, if you'd prefer—"

The bell on the door out front jingled. Trish and Nadia looked at each other, both of them holding baking trays in their hands and with four more on the counter that needed to be loaded up and put in the ovens.

"Shoot," Trish muttered, peeking into the front of the bakery. "There's a whole group of them out there. I've got a cake to make, a batch of brownies to mix, and not enough hands to do it. Can you help them?"

It was becoming more and more common for them to have to scramble to keep up with both the demands of the counter out front and the duties of the kitchen, which was good, but…. "I think it's time," Nadia said solemnly.

Trish's eyes widened. "Holy—you think so?"

"I do."

They stared at each other. "Help-wanted ad in the paper or sign in the window?" Trish asked finally.

"Let's try both."

Both women whooped with delight at the same time, and no doubt they made an interesting picture as they tried to hug each other without dropping any trays or scones.

"Girlfriend," Nadia added, feeling a sudden wave of optimism despite the stint of childcare in her near future, "I think this might just be our year."

❖ Chapter Three ❖

NADIA WASN'T LATE THIS time—not really—but Benji still beat her to the café where they planned to have lunch.

"I'll bet you're early to every single meeting you go to," she said by way of greeting, unable to resist teasing him. It was the suit and tie, she supposed. A girl couldn't be expected to resist trying to loosen a guy like him up a little bit. "Aren't you?"

He immediately rose from his chair and didn't sit down again until Nadia was seated. "Not *every* meeting."

She gave him a knowing look, and he momentarily averted his eyes. "Liar. It's okay, though. Women much prefer a man who's early to one who keeps them waiting."

"Ah, yes, well…speaking of that—" Benji cleared his throat and played with the knot of his tie as if it were too tight. "I know Mrs. Beasley means well, but I can't help but feel a little silly here."

"And you want to tell her thanks but no thanks?"

"Something along those lines, yes."

"Good luck with that. If you figure out a way that works, will you let me know?"

"In fact, I probably would have canceled our lunch meeting today and spared us both the trouble, but you left the coffee shop pretty quickly yesterday, and I had no way of reaching you." The look he gave her might have been vaguely accusing, but he masked it well beneath a polite exterior.

"Oh, yeah. You caught that, did you?" She thought he didn't really look all that irritated to be here, though, and she was experienced enough with men to guess that it might have something to do with the way she was smiling at him. She was not a vain woman, but she knew men liked her smile, especially when she turned it on them full force. "Well, we're here now, so we might as well make the most of it." Waving over a young waiter with a crew cut who beamed back at her, Nadia gave her order. "Hi, there. Can I get a turkey on rye and a hot tea, please?" She turned to her reluctant companion. "What about you?"

"What? Oh. Roast beef, please. On wheat. And just water for me."

The waiter departed, leaving Nadia and Benji to study each other. He seemed…not wary, exactly, she decided. More like he still wasn't sure what to make of the whole situation, or of her. That was perfectly understandable, but hopefully he wouldn't turn skittish and flee, because she was growing increasingly curious about what exactly lay beneath his polished surface. "So, are you saying you don't need any help with your love life? Most men do, you know. No shame in admitting it."

"I'm not—I don't—" Benji sputtered, and then he took a deep breath and tried again. "I'm just saying that I'm not sure where she got the idea that I'm in trouble when it comes to my social life."

"You're not wearing a wedding ring. Mrs. B sees that kind of thing as a cry for help. Trust me, I know. She gives me a hard time about that, too."

Benji's gaze dropped to Nadia's left hand, and for some reason the curiosity behind his eyes made her feel self-conscious. She dropped her hands into her lap and cleared her throat.

"Do you have a girlfriend?" she asked bluntly to steer the conversation firmly away from herself and back on track.

He blinked. "No."

"Boyfriend?"

"What? No! I just work a lot, that's all." He was turning pink again.

Nadia was delighted. She was going to have so much fun with him, if she could only convince him to let her.

"Makes it hard to meet people that way," he continued, "but I really don't need to be your charity case, Miss Nor—"

She raised one eyebrow.

"Nadia," he amended. "Really. I appreciate your offer, but I'm fine."

Great. She'd come on too strong and bruised his ego. But clearly he needed her help. No one who was too busy to get out and meet people was fine, not unless they aspired to be a hermit. This man was sorely in need of a social lifeline, even if he couldn't seem to see it. "New Year's Eve is just around the corner, you know," she pointed out. "Biggest social time of the year. Going to any parties?"

"I—there's a work thing, yes," he answered, and she could have sworn she heard a note of defensiveness in his voice.

Work?

Her dismay must have showed on her face, because he began fidgeting with his tie again.

Play nice, she told herself. "Okay. So, any ladies at work you've got your eye on? I'll bet I can help you get that midnight kiss."

He blinked at her but didn't respond.

Either there was no lady on the horizon, or she needed to prove his need for her help some other way. "I tell you what, I'll make you a deal. You tell me your moves when it comes to women, and if they're solid, I'll walk out of here and tell Mrs. B that her worries are for nothing. Sound fair?"

"My moves? Are you serious?"

"As a heart attack." Nadia leaned back to allow the approaching waiter room to slide her sandwich and tea in front f her. "Go ahead. Pick me up."

Benji stared at her and then seemed to notice that the waiter hadn't moved and was watching them both with new interest. "Thank you," he told the young man pointedly, glancing at the sandwich that was still in the waiter's hand. "You can go now."

Grinning, the waiter set the sandwich before Benji and sidled away with a backward glance and what sounded suspiciously like a snicker.

"I can't pick you up *now*," Benji insisted, lowering his voice and glancing around the café. "Not here, not like this."

"Sure you can. Here, I'll set the scene." Nadia crossed her legs and let the high heel boot of the top one sway flirtatiously as she gave Benji a coy look. "You're out for lunch. You're walking though a deli and suddenly you spot your dream girl sitting alone at a table. What do you do?"

He opened his mouth to speak, but nothing came out.

"Well, you'd better say something, honey. If you just stand there and stare at her like that, she'll either think you're having a seizure or she'll mace you. Just say the first thing that pops into your head."

"I feel ridiculous," he muttered.

"All right, try saying the second thing," she said wryly. "Come on, it's not ridiculous, it's practical. If you can't say it to me, how do you expect to say it to the woman of your dreams? Go ahead, what would you say?"

Gesturing helplessly, Benji shrugged. "Hi?"

It was about as basic as one could get but still workable as long as he could follow it up with something decent. Playing her part of the dream girl in question, Nadia gave him a dazzling smile. "Well, hi there." She leaned forward in invitation, more than a little curious to see what his next move would be.

Benji's gaze dropped to her lips as she smiled, and he froze.

Nadia cocked her head at him and waited some more, but it didn't seem as if he had anything else to say. She resisted the urge to shake her head. "'Hi' is good for starters, but it won't get you far unless you follow it up with something else real quick. So…?"

He turned his attention to his sandwich. "I forget," he muttered, and he took a bite instead.

"Hi, my name's Benji. Hi, mind if I join you? Hi, that's a lovely sweater you're wearing. Any of those would work just fine, trust me. You don't need to overthink it. Mostly women are going to feel flattered you approached them. As long as you respect their boundaries," she added, suddenly picturing him going overboard with an unsuspecting girl and having things not end well. "Otherwise you're looking at mace again."

He only grunted in response and continued chewing.

Was she losing his interest, or winning him over? It was hard to tell. Perhaps he still questioned her credibility. "Say she gives you the green light, she's smiling at you—and maybe she's even invited you to join her. Now what?"

"I'd tell her there's a little old lady who desperately wants to see me get married, and is she interested?"

The unexpected hint of humor caught her off guard, and this time she was the one who blinked in surprise.

He noticed. "What? I prefer the honest approach," he said around another bite.

Her lips twitched, and finally she allowed herself to smile. "I like you," she said after a minute.

He paused in his chewing as if startled by her admission.

Well, it wasn't the first time her candidness had caught someone off guard, and it was a safe bet that it wouldn't be the last, either. Nadia leaned forward. "Look, If you'd really rather drop all this because it's just a pain in your behind, I'll do it. I can't promise you that Mrs. B won't redouble her efforts—and God knows what form it will take—but I'll bow out. But if you even just give me a week, I'll bet I can help you."

Benji stared at her and then finally swallowed his bite of food. "Why?"

"Because I know what women look for in a man."

"No, I mean, why do you want to do this?"

"I like you," she repeated, and she did. Far more than she'd expected to when Mrs. B had set all of this up. "And I like seeing people get their happy endings. What can I say? I'm a romantic."

"I see." Those bright blue eyes of his seemed to focus on her just a little bit more than they had a moment ago. "So does that mean you've already got your happy ending?"

For a moment she didn't know how to answer. "Oh, don't worry about me, honey," she said finally with more lightness than she felt and a flippant smile. "I've got all the romance I can handle right now. My dance card couldn't be any more full."

"Oh?"

She ignored the question in his voice and took a sip of her tea.

After a long moment, Benji put down his sandwich and cleared his throat. "Look, it's nice of you to offer, Miss—Nadia, but I think I'm going to have to decline. I'm not quite as hard up as Mrs. B seems to think."

Time to pull out the big guns. "You do know she has access to a marriage broker, don't you? A real live marriage broker. I've seen the woman in action. She's got a stack of prospect photos as thick as my arm." It was a slight exaggeration, but only very slight. "I'm saying this because I feel it's only fair to warn you. If you turn me down, that's what Mrs. B may surprise you with next."

He looked horrified. "She wouldn't."

"Wouldn't she?" Nadia upped the wattage of her smile. "Suddenly a week with me doesn't sound so bad now, does it? So what's it going to be? Do I stay, or do I go?"

He said nothing at first, but then he finally sighed and threw his hands up into the air. "Stay."

"Good, because I probably wouldn't have left anyway," she admitted.

Benji raised his eyebrows.

She smiled back.

CHRISTINE S. FELDMAN

❖ Chapter Four ❖

"YOUR MISSION, SHOULD YOU choose to accept it—and you really have no choice, so just go with it—is to leave here today with a woman's phone number."

"You do realize that I have a job to get back to, right? My lunch break ends in ten minutes."

"Stay focused. *This* is your job today," Nadia returned in a tone that left no room for argument.

"Tell that to the man who signs my paychecks—Hey, what are you doing?"

"Giving you a thirty-second makeover. Hold still." Nadia undid Benji's tie and stuffed it into his suit pocket before stripping the suit jacket off him, then proceeded to undo the top button of his dress shirt and roll up his sleeves.

He made a funny little sound under his breath.

"What?" she asked, pausing.

"Oh, nothing. I'm just not used to having a woman strip me in public, that's all."

"You should be so lucky, honey," she returned, amused but undeterred. "Listen, no woman will give you her phone number if you look like an auditor from the IRS." She took a step back to study him. Better, but maybe one or two more things… "Are those glasses absolutely essential?" she asked, removing them to see how he looked without them.

He immediately plucked them out of her hands and put them back on. "If I want to avoid inadvertently wandering into traffic and getting killed, yes."

"Fine, point taken. But the hair—" Nadia tousled it roughly with her fingers.

Benji started at the contact.

"Relax. I promise you're in good hands." There was something endearing about his uneasiness, though, and she gentled the motions of her fingers to appease him.

"My boss is going to think I got jumped by street thugs and mugged. On the plus side, maybe he'll think that's why I'm late getting back from lunch and excuse me."

"You don't look like you got mugged." Nadia took a step back and let her gaze travel up the full length of him. "You look good."

And he did, too. He still looked neat and trim overall, but he looked far more approachable now. Geek chic, Nadia thought, pleased. Without the suit jacket covering him up, it was obvious now that while Benji might be lean, he wasn't scrawny.

Benji's dark hair, mussed just enough, and those wide blue eyes that looked just a little bit shell-shocked gave him an endearing sort of lost-puppy look that even made her own pulse flutter for a moment.

"Oh, yeah," she assured him. "Much better. Trust me."

"Jury's still out on that. Now what?"

Now it was time for him to practice. "Follow me." Nadia led him out of the café where they had been eating and into a bookstore two buildings down. "A bookstore is a safe place to start. If you can't think of anything to say, all you have to do is look around and make a comment about one of the books nearby." She lowered her voice as they wandered further into the store, and then she spotted a young woman browsing. "There, target acquired. Up ahead on the left."

"The woman in the suede skirt?"

"She's perfect. Now remember what I told you: eye contact, be breezy, friendly—."

"She's really not my type."

"For the purpose of today's exercise, that doesn't matter worth beans. You're asking for her phone number, not her hand in marriage."

"Nadia, I'm not sure—"

"Marriage broker," she reminded him. "I kid you not."

He muttered something under his breath but made no more protests.

"Good." She gave him a nudge in the direction of the suede-skirted woman. "Go on, you can do this."

Sighing, Benji trudged off toward the blonde as if he was headed to the guillotine.

It was hard not to smile. Nadia did her best to hide that fact by grabbing a book from a nearby shelf and holding it up before her face as if she was reading it, and then she turned a surreptitious gaze in Benji's direction. He gave her a backward glance, and she waved him onward with an encouraging nod and a furtive little flick of her hand.

As Benji approached the blonde, the woman shifted her weight from one leg to the other and inadvertently turned her back to him as she flipped through a book. He stopped in his tracks, then took a deep breath and circled around to the other side where he made a rather poor show of pretending to examine the shelves nearest to him before clearing his throat loud enough that even Nadia had no trouble hearing it from a distance.

Ouch.

The blonde jumped and looked up, and Benji nodded at her with a smile. She nodded back with what might have been a trace of a smile herself, but then she immediately returned to her reading.

Not bad though, Nadia thought, trying not to wince. At least he'd managed to make first contact.

She saw him open his mouth then, presumably to introduce himself, and gesture at the bookshelf before them both.

The woman's eyes widened, and she shook her head curtly before hastening away and out of sight.

Nadia blinked. What on earth…?

Benji looked bewildered himself. Then he glanced at the bookshelf and did a double take before jerking back as if it had burned him.

Shoving her book back into its place, Nadia hurried over to him. "What did you just say to her?"

"I asked her if she had any favorites she could recommend to me," he said, his cheeks bright with color.

CHRISTINE S. FELDMAN

"Well, that doesn't seem so—" Nadia caught sight of the category label on the edge of the shelf. SEXUALITY. "Oh." She started to laugh, got a dirty look from Benji, and clapped a hand over her mouth to try to smother the sound.

"Would you please stop laughing? She's probably gone to tell the manager there's a pervert loose in his store."

"I'm sorry," she said, knowing she couldn't possibly sound sincere when she was still so obviously fighting laughter but unable to help herself. He frowned at her, but his miffed expression only served to add to his adorableness quotient. "Really, I'm sorry. Let's try it again, okay? But this time we'll pick a section that's more you."

"Finance," Benji said immediately.

"Not finance," Nadia objected almost as quickly. "How many love stories do you know of that started out with 'we met in the finance section'? You need something with at least the potential for romance."

"*Personal* finance?"

She groaned inwardly. "Come on, dig deeper. You've got hobbies, right? We could try books about one of those—unless it's Star Trek or something like that. I don't want to see you trying to hit on a woman in some pseudo-alien language."

"I am not a Trekkie," Benji told her, sounding aggrieved.

44

"Okay, fine." She turned her attention to the large category signs overhead in the bookstore. "Something else that would be more appropriate for—"

"You know," he interrupted her, "you could always just *say* you'd tutored me, or whatever we're calling this. Mrs. Beasley would never know the difference."

"You think I would lie to her? I think I might be insulted."

"I think you might be faking."

To a certain extent she was, yes, but she was reluctant to put an end to their fledgling acquaintance just yet, and she had a sneaking suspicion that he wasn't quite so opposed to all of this as he let on anyway. "You agreed to a week," she reminded him.

He snorted. "Only because you used scare tactics."

"One more," she cajoled. "Just try one more, and I promise we'll call it quits for the day."

"One more," he agreed finally, sighing.

"Okay, so how about..."

"How about travel?"

She turned and gave him an appraising look, wondering if he was just grasping at straws or if he really had ventured out to see foreign places. "Travel? That's not bad, Benji. Faraway places, exotic settings… I think we have a winner. Come on." And she headed toward the travel section in the bookstore, motioning for him to follow.

"You're enjoying this all way too much," he said, but he followed her. Unfortunately, the only woman browsing in the travel section when they got there was one who couldn't have been much younger than Mrs. B. "Well, we tried," Benji said, growing more cheerful, and he turned as if to leave.

Nadia put her hand on her arm to stop him. "Wait—"

A young redhead wandered past them and toward the Great Britain shelf, where she paused and pulled out a book to examine it.

"Perfect," Nadia said with satisfaction. She nudged Benji. "And may I suggest that this time you don't try to get her opinions on sexual practices."

"Thank you, that's very helpful."

"You're welcome."

He gave her a look but then manfully made his way over to stand beside the redhead, and after a moment, he spoke to her. She glanced at him and smiled at whatever he said, and he turned to face her more directly before speaking again.

Progress. Apparently he was a quick study.

But before Nadia could feel too pleased about her new pupil's progress, the redhead quirked her eyebrows and glanced in Nadia's direction before shaking her head and saying something that made Benji blink. Then the woman put the book she'd been holding back on the shelf and wandered off in the opposite direction.

"At least this one didn't sprint," Nadia observed when Benji returned to where she waited for him. "What did she just say to you?"

"That she's not into threesomes."

It was Nadia's turn to do a double take. "She thought you and I—"

He nodded.

"No…"

"Yes."

She didn't know whether to laugh or cry and wondered just how close he was to bolting out the door now. "At least she smiled at you before she made up her mind that you were kinky," she noted finally, trying to find something with which to encourage him. "That's a good sign, Benji. We're moving in the right direction."

"Absolutely, if the right direction includes a sexual harassment suit. They're going to slap up warning posters of me all around this place." Benji glanced at his watch. "But right now I'd better move in the direction of my office," he continued, rolling his shirtsleeves back down and buttoning their cuffs. "This was… interesting."

"You know, you actually did very well," she told him, meaning it.

"I'm sorry, which fish out of water were *you* watching?"

"No, really, you did. You just had a little bad luck with the circumstances, that's all. But you've got guts, Benji Garner. That's a very attractive quality in a man." It was a nice change from the machismo that most men she knew seemed to think qualified as the real thing.

"Mm," was all he said in response. Holding up his suit jacket, Benji fished around in the pockets until he found his tie. He slung the jacket over his arm and wrapped the tie around his neck, attempting to recreate the earlier knot with little success.

"Here, let me." Nadia loosened the clumsy knot he'd made, and Benji let his hands drop away as she took over. "So did today scare you off, or are you still in?" she asked, concentrating on the tie. There was no reply, so she glanced up and found him watching her.

He cleared his throat. "Depends. Does lesson two involve awkward bookstore scenarios in any way whatsoever?"

"Nope. It'll be safe, I promise."

"You know, it's funny, but I seem to remember you calling bookstores safe, too."

"They are. Today was just…fluke-ish."

"I'm not sure that's a word."

"Do I look worried?" She finished fixing his tie and smoothed it down. "Lesson two will be on dressing for success. In the dating world, at least. We can meet at your place. Safe enough?"

"It sounds safe," he agreed, "but then again, don't most ambushes seem that way at first?"

"Poor baby, so suspicious. It will get easier, you know." She patted his chest where his tie rested. "I am dying to see if there's anything else in your closet besides suits. Tomorrow night work for you?"

He slipped the suit jacket on. "I think so, but I'll have to check my calendar to be sure."

"All right, here." Nadia fished out one of the bakery business cards she carried around in her purse and scribbled down her cell phone number. "Call me when you know for sure," she told him, handing the card over.

"I will."

Hooking her arm through his, Nadia led the way toward the exit. "And I really mean it, Benji. You did great today. Just because you struck out—"

"I didn't strike out."

She stared at him as he held the door open for her, wondering how to politely remind him that he'd done exactly that, and not once but twice. "You didn't—"

Benji held up the card with her phone number on it.

Nadia blinked.

His eyes were wide with innocence, but there was the faintest hint of mischief in them. It was unexpectedly appealing. "Call you later," he said with a nod goodbye, and then he turned and walked off down the street.

And a bemused Nadia watched him leave as a slow smile formed on her lips.

❖ Chapter Five ❖

SEVERAL HOURS LATER, NADIA found herself sitting cross-legged on the floor of Ian's living room and across from his six-year-old daughter Kelsey, painting the little girl's fingernails with a bottle of plum-colored nail polish Nadia had found in the bottom of her purse.

"Pretty," Kelsey declared, holding up all ten of her fingers and eyeing them with approval.

"Glad you like it. Careful—don't smudge them. Blow on them for a couple of minutes," Nadia advised, putting the top back on the bottle. Nail polish. Who would have thought? After nearly twenty minutes of eyeing each other and Kelsey shooting down every activity Nadia suggested, it had been Revlon to the rescue.

"You work with Trish at her bakery," Kelsey said abruptly, confirming rather than asking.

"Yes, I do."

There was a gleam in the girl's eye as she lowered her voice conspiratorially.

"My dad likes Trish a lot."

Nadia grinned. "Trish likes him a lot, too. Sh, don't tell her I told you."

The girl nodded, apparently pleased with Nadia's response. "She's my dad's girlfriend now."

"Uh huh." Nadia plopped a couch pillow on the floor in front of her and patted it with one hand in invitation. "Here. Turn around, and I'll braid your hair." They'd have a full-fledged salon going here by the time Trish and Ian returned from the movie, but judging by the expression on her face, Kelsey was enjoying every minute of the attention.

The child settled onto the pillow with her back to Nadia, still admiring her newly-painted fingernails. "You're really pretty. Do you have a boyfriend, too?" she asked over her shoulder.

Nadia began combing Kelsey's hair through her fingers. "I have lots of boyfriends."

"Lots?" the girl repeated in such a tone that Nadia didn't need to see her face to know she had screwed it up into an "are you nuts" kind of expression. "Aren't you just supposed to have one?"

"Different strokes for different folks."

"What does that mean?"

"It means not everybody does things the same way."

"So you like all your boyfriends the way Trish likes my dad?"

Nadia's fingers slowed in their braiding. "Well, no," she said after a moment, considering her answer and the best way to deliver it to a six-year-old girl. "It's more like they're—I mean… well, it's sort of like getting to meet all kinds of exciting new friends. It's just fun, that's all, sweetie. And it keeps life interesting."

"My dad and Trish have fun."

"That's true," Nadia admitted, biting back a smile. "But it's a different kind of fun."

"How?"

Nothing like getting grilled about one's relationship status by a gradeschooler, Nadia thought. "Well, it just is."

Kelsey drew a deep breath, and Nadia suspected she was about to ask another question about her love life.

"Braid's done," she said quickly before Kelsey could speak. Turning the girl around to face her, Nadia smiled a little too brightly. "Tell you what. If we can change the subject to anything else in the world, I'll paint your toenails, too. Deal?"

Kelsey's eyes brightened. "Deal."

Yes, Nadia thought with relief. She was going to have to write a thank-you letter to Revlon very soon. "Great. What shall we talk about next?" she asked as she retrieved the bottle of nail polish.

The little girl smiled a beatific smile. "Do you like zombies?"

Nadia blinked.

◆ ◆ ◆

"So Gram says you're going to turn Benji Garner into a ladies' man."

Nadia poked her head out of the kitchen to see Aimee Beasley standing at the bakery counter near Trish. Gone was the goth look and the jet-black hair. Now the young woman sported a warm honey-colored blonde that was probably a lot closer to her natural hair color. Well, except for the pink streak running through one lock of it. "She does, does she? Did she tell you how she set it up?"

Aimee snorted. "She didn't have to. I've seen her when she's in guilt-trip mode. Suckered you with the whole trembling voice and teary eyes thing, didn't she?" The girl rested on one elbow and eyed a tray of cupcakes that Trish was in the process of frosting.

"Something like that." And yet, Nadia wasn't quite as irritated now with Mrs. B as she had been before.

"Doesn't work on me anymore since I go with her to all of her doctors' appointments. She's healthier than any of us, trust me."

"Somehow I'm not surprised."

Aimee drew just a little bit closer to the cupcakes. "So you think you can do something with him, huh?"

"Oh, absolutely." Feeling the effects of having been on her feet all day, Nadia leaned against the doorframe to rest her back. "There's lots of potential there, once I get him loosened up a little."

Trish looked up from her frosting. "She's enjoying herself," she told Aimee. "Did you see the way her eyes lit up just now? Poor guy's like her lab rat."

"He is not," Nadia returned. "I'm not experimenting on him, I'm helping him."

"So what's the plan?" Aimee asked her. "Give him a head-to-toe makeover, a pair of contact lenses, and turn him loose on the women of the world?"

"He says contacts are a no-go. Doesn't want to put anything on his eyeball."

Nadia grimaced. "Can't say I blame him there. But tonight I am going to give him a lesson on wardrobe and grooming."

"Tonight?" Trish repeated, glancing up at her.

"Sure. Why not tonight?"

Trish took a break from her cupcakes and turned around, massaging the muscles in her neck. "It's just—it's Saturday. I thought you liked to hit the clubs on Saturday nights."

Funny, but that had slipped her mind somehow. Nadia shrugged and waved a hand in dismissal. "There's always next week for that. We made a deal: one week. New Year's Eve is coming up, and I'm trying to get him ready."

"You make it sound like an unveiling."

"Kind of. With a little effort, I think Benji's going to turn a few heads."

"No doubt he's delighted."

"Not as much as you'd think, no. Well, he's a man. What do men know about style and charm anyway?"

"I thought you said the right kinds of men knew *everything* about it," Trish said wryly.

"And with my help, Benji will join their ranks," Nadia said, switching gears and refusing to be fazed by it. She straightened, ready to return to the kitchen.

"Whether he wants to or not."

"I heard that," Nadia shot back.

Trish grinned. "You were supposed to."

Aimee's voice startled them both. "Hey, what do you guys think?"

They turned and saw Aimee putting the finishing touches on the rest of the cupcakes.

"So," she said, holding up the tube of frosting and examining the results of her handiwork with satisfaction. "I hear you're hiring."

◆ ◆ ◆

NADIA STEPPED OFF THE elevator in Benji's apartment building and glanced at the slip of paper in her hand to double check his address. "Apartment four-oh-four," she said aloud, and then she turned her head and saw his door to her left. Worn out as she was from a busy day of work, she found herself perking up in anticipation of the evening's events, and she raised her hand to knock briskly on Benji's door.

He opened it almost immediately. "Hi," he greeted her, and then he glanced at his watch with feigned shock. "I must be rubbing off on you. You're early."

"I find being late a few times makes people appreciate it all the more when I'm early."

"Good strategy." Benji opened the door wider and stood to one side to let her enter.

His apartment was a lot like him, Nadia decided as she stepped inside. Not flashy but neat and orderly.

There was no dirty laundry lying about or any evidence of used dishes stacked in the sink, which were things she had come to expect from most men who were bachelors. Oh, there were a few things out—a glass on the coffee table with a dog-eared paperback beside it, a couple of remotes for an impressive entertainment system, and what looked like a day's worth of unopened mail—but nothing that could be called clutter.

"Baseball fan, huh?" she asked, catching sight of a framed jersey hanging on his wall.

He nodded. "You?"

"I wouldn't even know which end of the bat to hold," she admitted wryly.

"Nothing a day at the batting cage can't fix."

"Batting cage? Me?" She raised an eyebrow. "Not likely."

"Ah, so you can tell me to try new things, but I can't do the same for you?" Now he raised *his* eyebrows, and she could have sworn she saw a hint of the same mischief she'd seen when they parted ways at the bookstore.

"Touché," she conceded, inclining her head in acknowledgment. Turning, she dropped her purse on the kitchenette table beside where his suit jacket hung over the back of a chair. "Clean kitchen," she observed immediately, which might have been due to the baker in her. Compared to the ones she'd seen in most bachelor pads, his kitchen practically beckoned her into it. "What a guy. Does housework, has a steady job—"

"I floss, too."

"I'm telling you, Benji, you are turning out to be quite the catch. If you can rotate tires and give decent foot massages, I'll marry you myself."

"Sorry," he said, putting a hand to his heart as if pained. "But I have it on good authority that by New Year's Eve I'm going to be irresistible to women everywhere, so I have to keep my options open."

Nadia grinned. "Benji Garner, you are a player."

"Yeah, I get that a lot."

She studied him with a growing appreciation. He was proving to be not at all what she'd expected him to be, and she was increasingly curious to find out what other surprises were in store. "Come on," she said, nudging him with her shoulder. "Show a girl what's inside your closet."

❖ Chapter Six ❖

"NOT BAD, BENJI," NADIA called out as she combed through the shirts hanging on his closet rack. Sure, there were plenty of suits and ties, but there were actual honest-to-goodness street clothes in there, too. "I'm actually a little bummed we won't need to go on a shopping spree. I was looking forward to trying Armani on you."

"I think I just heard my credit cards gasp in relief." Benji's voice traveled in to her from the living room. "Do you like Thai food?"

"Love it. Why?"

"I'm ordering in. No man should have to learn how to color coordinate on an empty stomach. Pad Thai okay with you? And fried rice?"

"Sure, thanks."

"Shrimp or chicken with the rice?"

"Chicken." She pulled out a blue dress shirt that she suspected would make his eyes dazzle and turned around when Benji finally entered the room. "All right, I need a white t-shirt and jeans, stat."

"Yes, Ma'am," Benji replied gravely, retrieving the requested items from his bureau and holding them up.

"Perfect. Go try these on, and I'll see what else I can put together," Nadia said as she began taking inventory of his t-shirts. "There aren't any dirty little secrets I'm going to stumble onto in your dresser drawers, are there?"

"Are you talking about private papers or more like something in sequins?" he called out from the adjoining bathroom as he disappeared into it.

She let out a startled chuckle. "Both, I guess."

"No, you're fine."

He really had been remarkably agreeable about all of this. Trish had been right when she'd said Nadia was enjoying herself, and she felt a flicker of guilt now that perhaps she had assumed too much when she told herself Benji didn't really mind her jumping in this way.

"Benji," Nadia said after a minute, slowing in her movements as she laid out pieces of clothing on his plain navy-colored bedspread.

"Yes?"

"Am I being too pushy? You can say so if I am."

"Pushy? No," he said through the door.

"Are you sure?" It was completely natural for Nadia to come on strong. Her mother was quite fond of reminding her that she was born in the middle of hurricane season and seemed to have absorbed the force of at least one of the storms. But as the circumstances of the present situation sank in to her, Nadia realized it *was* the first time she had ever found herself in the bedroom of a man she'd met such a short time ago—rearranging his wardrobe, no less.

"Yes, I'm sure. Although if I walk in there and find you elbow deep in my underwear drawer, I reserve the right to change my opinion."

Her lips twitched. "Fair enough. But just so you know, this is kind of a first, even for me."

"Well...for me, too. So I guess that makes us even."

"You're a sweet guy, Benji. You know that?"

"So my mother tells me. She'll be thrilled to have her opinion verified by an outside source." Benji emerged from the bathroom then, jean-clad and tucking in the hem of the dress shirt.

63

"No, don't tuck," Nadia told him, putting her hand on his to stop him. "Tucking is fine for formal occasions, but trust me. Leave it out."

He momentarily stilled as she touched him, and then he cleared his throat and followed her instructions.

"Much better. And I think we ought to undo one more button at the top—there you go." Nadia took a step back to admire him, and her lips parted in a smile of pure pleasure. "Oh, I was so right about that shirt with your eyes. Blue is definitely your color. Here, take a look at yourself." Putting her hands on his shoulders, she turned him toward the mirror that was attached to his dresser. "See?"

"Stunning," he said wryly. "I even take my own breath away."

Men, she thought, resisting the urge to roll her eyes. Did he really not notice the difference? And did he really not realize the kind of appeal he held? Apparently not, because even now his gaze rested more on her reflection in the mirror than on his own. "And if we roll up the sleeves," she continued, undeterred, "it's even better. Good forearms look great on a man—hey, do you work out?" she asked, feeling his arms for a moment and marveling.

"I play racquetball with some of my clients," he answered, and it might have been her imagination, but for a moment she could have sworn his voice took on a slightly strained note.

"Oh?"

"Yes. Mrs. Beasley wipes the floor with me every time."

Nadia did a double take. "You're kidding."

"Yes, I am."

"A comedian, huh?" She gave him a little shove. "Come on, back to business." But her eyes inadvertently dropped to his jeans. He filled them out surprisingly well. Maybe she ought to look into racquetball herself if it got results like that. Realizing just where her gaze was lingering, she forced her eyes upward. "Okay, time to talk color palettes. Now there are warm skin tones and cool skin tones, and yours is definitely cool. There are going to be some colors that compliment it, and some that really don't, so—"

"Color palettes?" he interrupted, sounding aghast as he turned around. "Dear God. Are you serious?"

"Yes, and after I explain how they work, I'm going to give you a pop quiz to see if you can match appropriate pieces of clothing."

"There's going to be a quiz? I take it back. You are pushy."

"Too late, honey. Now you should probably write this stuff down so you'll remember it." Nadia smiled at him. "Got a pencil?"

◆ ◆ ◆

FORTY MINUTES LATER, BENJI was both paying the deliveryman who had brought their food and

65

simultaneously refusing the cash Nadia was trying to give him for her share.

"I can't," he told her with a pained expression on his face as he closed the door. "My mother would disown me for taking money from a guest in my home. You wouldn't want to break up a family, would you?"

"If I'm eating, I should be paying, too," she objected.

"Don't make me get my mother on the phone."

"Maybe I'll call that bluff. What's she like?"

"Absolutely terrifying."

"Ha! *Your* mother? I don't believe you."

"Good. You really shouldn't. Actually," Benji said as he unpacked to-go boxes of food from the delivery bag and set them on the kitchen counter, "she's warmhearted, generous to a fault, and the kind of person who will refill somebody's plate anytime she sees it's empty—whether they like it or not. So you can understand why I have to represent well here. Plate?" he asked, offering one.

She took it. "Thanks."

"That's even how she met my father. They worked in the same office but never met until one day she passed his desk, noticed the sad excuse for a lunch he brought, and informed him that was no way to eat. She brought him something the next day, and then the next after that, and so on. My father deliberately brought crackers and apples for days just to keep her coming by until he got up the nerve to ask her out."

Nadia smiled at him. "Smooth operator, your father."

"Well, it's worked out pretty well for them. Been married over thirty years, and they still dote on each other."

"Really? Wow."

"What about your folks? No, wait—let me guess. Social expertise runs in the family, and one of them picked the other up with an unforgettable line. Am I right?"

A memory played through her mind of her parents bitterly arguing, one of many. Nadia's smile faded. "I don't really know," she said, turning away and pretending to examine a DVD shelf in Benji's living room. "Anyway, they split up a long time ago."

"I'm sorry." Benji said immediately. "None of my business."

"Forget it, ancient history," she assured him, shrugging with a nonchalance that was more feigned than she'd expected it to be. Searching for a change in topic, she zeroed in on one of his DVDs. "Oh, boy. Busted."

"Who, me? For what?"

Nadia pulled out the DVD and held it up. "I thought you said you weren't a Trekkie."

"That's Star *Wars* you're holding there, not Star *Trek*," he informed her.

"Is there a difference?"

Benji's eyes widened, and he clutched at his chest as if wounded.

"What? They're both about people flying around in outer space, right?"

"That's like saying Blazing Saddles is the same as Dances With Wolves because they both have people riding horses. Have you never watched Star Wars?"

She shrugged and shook her head.

"Not even once? How is that possible?"

"If it's not a chick-flick, I don't watch it. Unless Denzel Washington's involved," she clarified. "For him, I make an exception."

"That's rather limiting, isn't it?" Benji observed, pouring her a glass of water. "Trust me, Stars Wars is universal. Men, women…old, young…doesn't matter. There's something in it for everyone. It's got adventure, drama, humor—epic good versus evil, family relationships, and maybe even a few life lessons. Whereas Star Trek is more about a certain ship's captain extending the hand of friendship to every female alien he meets, if you know what I mean. Got it? Or maybe you should write all of this down so you'll remember it." He gave her a sideways glance and held out the glass in his hand. "Got a pencil?"

He had that look down very well, Nadia thought as she took the glass from him, and the fact that he didn't seem to realize how charming it was made it all the more effective on him. "That won't be necessary."

"Pop it into the machine," Benji suggested with a nod toward his DVD player. "We'll let the movie speak for itself."

"What? It's, like, two hours long, isn't it? I can't stay that late." And yet even as she glanced at her watch, Nadia found herself—much to her surprise—tempted.

His gaze dropped from her to the box of food he was opening "Hot date, huh?"

"No, nothing like that."

He perked up again.

"Early shift at the bakery," Nadia explained, but even she could hear her voice wavering with indecision.

Benji eyed her and waited.

"Would there be popcorn involved?" she asked finally.

"There can be."

"Buttered?"

"Is there any other way?"

After a moment, she nodded. "All right, I'm in."

A grin of unabashed pleasure spread across Benji's face, one that sent an unexpected tingle down Nadia's spine. "You won't regret it. Forty-seven percent of all pop culture references made in the world today are about Star Wars, and now you'll finally be able to get them."

"Forty-seven percent?" she returned, trying to ignore the tingle. "You made that up."

"Yes, I did. Napkin?"

"Please."

And as she kicked off her shoes and settled in beside Benji on his couch to watch the movie, plate of food in hand and legs curled comfortably beneath her, it struck Nadia as ironic that she, Nadia Normandy, had not only agreed to an evening in of her own free will, but she was thoroughly enjoying it.

◆ ◆ ◆

IT MIGHT HAVE BEEN the crick in her neck that woke her up, but whatever it was that finally did it, it gradually brought Nadia back to awareness to the point where she realized her head was resting on something much too hard to be her pillow. It rose and fell ever so slightly, too, with the slow and even rhythm of a sleeper's breathing.

A shoulder.

Peeling her eyes open, Nadia first noticed the glow of the television screen that was on and was showing the Play Me screen of the Star Wars DVD. The only other light in the room came from a single lamp in the corner—they had decided to turn the others off for the movie, she remembered now—and it illuminated the room enough to remind her that she was in Benji's apartment, and that her head was resting on his shoulder.

Good grief, she thought foggily, trying to clear her head. She'd fallen asleep during the movie, hadn't she? No, wait, that wasn't quite right, because she remembered seeing the end of it. It must have happened after that. They'd been talking about something… He'd asked her about how she'd gotten into the bakery business, and she'd told him about some of the mishaps that had occurred along the way to opening Heavenly Bites with Trish. She'd been laughing and comfortable and cozy, and then she'd leaned back against the cushions, intending to close her eyes for just a minute…

Nadia raised her head carefully so as not to wake Benji and then winced sharply at the ache in her neck. It had been a long time since she'd fallen asleep in a position like this—leaning on someone else, no less—and now her neck felt like one of those twisty straws that children liked to use to sip their drinks. Rubbing the muscles in her neck with one hand, she turned to look over at Benji where he slept beside her on his couch. His head rested back against the cushions as his chest rose and fell with deep, even breaths, stretching the t-shirt he wore ever so slightly each time over his torso in a way that was not exactly unappealing.

Wow. Racquetball, she thought again. Really? Or maybe batting practice, too.

Benji mumbled something in his sleep, and Nadia started as she realized she'd been staring at him. He shifted position but didn't wake, and it occurred to her then that his previous position— while allowing her to rest her head on him in relative comfort—couldn't have been all that comfortable for him. And yet he hadn't tried to move her.

She felt a flicker of affection. He really was a very nice guy, and surprisingly easy to be around considering that it had only been three days since they'd met. Three days was barely enough time to scratch the surface with somebody, and yet here she was one pajama set away from having a slumber party at his place. That was very unlike her.

The slight movement he had made a moment ago was enough to leave Benji's glasses askew on his face. They'd no doubt be much safer on an end table than on his face while he was sleeping, especially if he rolled over and they slid off, so Nadia very carefully reached to lift the frames from off his face and set them aside, aware that she was removing them as much out of curiosity as concern for their safekeeping.

She'd known already that he had nice features, but they were even nicer without the glasses in their way. No chiseled edges maybe like you might see in the pages of a magazine, but still very appealing, especially with the hint of stubble that was there now. Disarming, even. The stubble was appealing, too, a sharp contrast to his usual tidy suit-and-tie image. It was a shame he didn't allow it to show more often. Maybe she should suggest it.

Another thought popped into her head then that made her forget Benji and instead scramble to check her watch. She bit back a curse as she saw the time. She was going to be late starting her shift at the bakery. Late was an understatement, actually, but as long as she didn't try to go home and change first—she grimaced, longing for a shower—at least she wouldn't be unforgivably late.

And as much as she was starting to like Benji, surely three days was not nearly a long enough time to know someone before asking to use his shower?

Moving cautiously so as not to disturb him with her movements, Nadia pushed herself up off the couch. For a moment she debated whether or not to nudge him awake and say goodbye, but he looked so adorably peaceful lying there that she finally decided against it. A note would do just as well, she supposed, her gaze lingering on him as her thoughts returned to their evening together.

She'd had a far better time than she'd expected—although she suspected that had more to do with the company than the movie.

"Sword-fighting with lasers? How is that even possible?" she'd demanded at one point, one hand reaching for popcorn

and the other gesturing at the television screen. "Wouldn't they just go right through each other?"

"You're completely missing the point," Benji told her.

"Which is?"

"That they're insanely awesome."

Nadia started to laugh. "How is that an argument?"

He stopped her mouth from saying anything further by popping a piece of popcorn into it. "Sh. It's rude to talk when the movie's on. Eat your popcorn."

Then she'd tossed a popped kernel at him, and he'd retaliated…

They had gone through two bowls of popcorn that way—there were still a few kernels lying around as evidence.

It was so completely not her style of fun. And she had so completely had a blast.

Would it be the same for Benji, she wondered, if he stepped into her world and tried it on for size? It would probably make a great next step for him to stretch the boundaries of his comfort zone. Dinner out at a trendy tapas bar, wine-tasting at a gallery of unconventional art, or maybe—

Maybe…

Oh, yes, Nadia thought as a third option came to mind, and her mouth curved upward in anticipation.

Grabbing an unused napkin from among the now empty takeout boxes, Nadia scribbled a hasty note and left it on the coffee table for Benji to find.

And then, with her mind still a little on the fuzzy side but growing ever more alert at the prospect of the evening she was planning, Nadia retrieved her purse and tiptoed out of the apartment.

CHRISTINE S. FELDMAN

❖ Chapter Seven ❖

NADIA POPPED A PAIR of baking sheets full of pastries into the ovens just as she heard Trish's key turn in the lock. "Morning," she offered briskly over her shoulder as she turned her attention to the next batch of dough on her list, still scrambling to get back on schedule.

"Morning," Trish echoed cheerfully from behind her. "Wow. Looks like a bag of flour exploded in—" Then she paused for a long moment before speaking again, her tone suddenly uncertain. "Um, Nadia?"

"Yes?"

"Am I crazy, or are those the same clothes you were wearing yesterday?"

"I'd say you're right on both counts," Nadia said, leaving her mixing bowl long enough to check on the status of the donuts that were rising in the corner. "But kooky as you are, I still love you."

"Mm. I'm laughing on the inside."

The donuts were doing fine. Another half an hour and she could slide them into the oven. "I never made it home last night," Nadia said, her mind preoccupied with her to-do list as she returned to her mixing. "No big deal. Pass me the baking powder, would you?"

"You never made it—what exactly happened yesterday?" Trish asked, handing her the baking powder as requested and hastily reaching for an apron.

"We went through Benji's closet, ordered in Thai food, and ended up watching a movie."

"And?"

"And I guess after being on my feet all day, I was just really tired. I fell asleep on his couch. Actually, we both did."

To her surprise, Trish started to laugh.

"What's so funny?"

"Nadia Normandy spending a Saturday night with take-out and a couch, that's what. Doesn't exactly fit your usual description of 'fun.' Must be slowing down in your old age, what with thirty on the horizon."

"Bite your tongue," Nadia told her, stirring in the baking powder. "And around here we say twenty-ten, woman."

"My apologies."

"That would sound a lot more sincere if you weren't smirking."

"Wouldn't it, though?" Trish reached for a mixing bowl of her own. "So what movie did you watch?"

"Star Wars."

Trish stared at her. "You did not."

"We did."

"Why? Did you think Denzel Washington was in it?"

"Ha ha. No. Benji said I ought to give it a chance, so I did."

"And?"

"Not bad," she admitted, avoiding Trish's eyes and beginning to feel a tad self-conscious.

"You not only watched Star Wars, but you *liked* it? And you stayed in on a Saturday night to do it?" Trish's eyes suddenly widened. "Isn't that one of the signs of the apocalypse?"

Nadia flashed her a dirty look. "Are you finished?"

"I don't know yet. I'll keep you posted."

"Hey, I never said I had anything against a quiet evening in."

"Ha! Yeah, right."

"I didn't!"

"Actions speak louder than words, babe," Trish told her with a pointed look. "And your actions have always screamed 'night on the town.'"

"I'm about to take an action with this spoon that you're not going to like much," Nadia said, holding up the wooden spoon in her hand warningly.

"You know, I think now might be a good time for me to refill the napkin dispensers out front," Trish said, backing away from Nadia with exaggerated care.

"Good idea," said Nadia, resuming her mixing.

◆ ◆ ◆

"THE DRAWER ON THE cash register sticks a bit sometimes, but if you jiggle it like this—" Nadia demonstrated while Aimee watched. "It loosens right back up again. See?"

"Got it," Aimee agreed.

Nadia made a sweeping gesture at the front counter and everything on it. "And that pretty much wraps up the basics for running the front. Other than that, smile at the customers and wipe down the tables when there's a lull. Any questions?"

"Sure. Hypothetical situation…"

"Yes?"

"Say I drop a scone or something on the floor but pick it up before any customers see it. Do you guys believe in the five-second rule, or not?"

Nadia stared at her. "Oh, honey, please tell me you're joking."

Aimee grinned.

"Yeah, you'll fit in just fine here," Nadia told the girl wryly just as her cell phone rang. "Trish, can you show Aimee how to work the alarm?" she called out as she pulled her phone from her pocket and pressed the talk button. "Hello?"

"You're trying to kill me, aren't you?"

The sound of Benji's voice on her phone sent a small thrill of pleasure through her. "Hi," she returned. "What's this about trying to kill you? I remember everyone I issue death threats to, and you're not on my list for today."

"No? That's pretty much what your note amounted to. Salsa dancing? Really?"

Nadia smiled. "Nobody dies from salsa dancing, Benji."

"What about the ones who die from shame?"

"Every man should learn a few dance steps to keep in his back pocket—especially if he's trying to learn how to sweep women off their feet."

"I might trip a few on the dance floor. Does that count as sweeping?"

"I'm sure you'll do better than that. Besides, you know what they say, Benji. What doesn't kill you makes you stronger. I promise I'll walk you through the steps. But women *love* a man who can dance, plus dance clubs are great places to meet new people, so will you at least try it?"

There was faint mumbling on the other end.

Nadia strained to hear. "What?"

"Nothing, I was just trying to bargain with God. Didn't work."

She bit back a laugh. "Pick me up at eight. I'll text you the address."

"You're a cruel woman, Nadia Normandy."

"Me? I'm as sweet as pumpkin pie. See you tonight, Benji."

"Fine. Eight o'clock."

Ending the call, Nadia shoved the phone back in her pocket with the unwavering feeling that—despite the fact that she always enjoyed dancing anyway—tonight was going to be a particularly interesting night.

◆ ◆ ◆

NADIA GLANCED AT THE clock on her wall and then returned her attention to her reflection in the mirror so she could finish putting on her lipstick. Knowing Benji, he would probably be early, so she was quick to apply the finishing touches before taking a step back and giving herself a final appraisal. Red was a good color for her, especially when it belonged to a flirty little dress that was perfect for salsa dancing. She'd chosen it after at least fifteen minutes of combing through her clothes, which was far more time than she usually spent picking out an outfit these days.

But after all, it was Benji's first time salsa dancing. Surely that warranted a little extra effort on her part?

There was a knock on her door, and she felt a flicker of anticipation. Benji Garner on a dance floor. This was going to truly be something to see.

She opened the door to find him standing out in the hallway, in the process of wiping his glasses on the hem of his shirt that he had, to his credit, remembered to leave untucked. "Hi," he greeted her as he started to put his glasses back on. "I know I'm a little early, but—" Then he stopped talking altogether as said glasses settled back onto the bridge of his nose and he caught sight of her.

Well, making a man speechless was as good a way as any to start off an evening, Nadia thought. "Hi."

Benji shook himself out of his apparent daze, but his expression was one of unabashed admiration. "Sorry, I swallowed my tongue for a minute there, but I'm better now. You look...stunning."

Yes, the red dress had been a good choice. "And you are getting better with small talk and flattery," she told him, pleased by his reaction. "You can never really go wrong with 'stunning'."

"It's only flattery if it isn't true, isn't it?"

"I think you're going to turn a few heads yourself tonight. You look *good*."

And he did. His coat was open at the front to reveal that Benji had taken her fashion advice to heart last night, because she recognized the shirt and slacks he had on as one combination she had shown him. They fit him well. Very well.

And his hair—it was ruffled and mussed just right, much as she had made it look that day at the bookstore. About the only thing he could have done to improve further on his look was to throw in the stubble that she'd admired on him last night. Or was it in the wee hours of the morning? In any case...

"Come on," she told Benji, slipping on her coat and reaching for her beaded clutch. "We look too good to waste another minute standing here. Let's go dance."

◆ ◆ ◆

LUNA BAILANDO WAS A popular hangout on any night, but with New Year's Eve as close as it was, there seemed to be even more revelers out than usual. Dancers already crowded the dance floor in the club, and virtually every seat in the place had already been claimed.

Benji said something from beside Nadia as they stood just inside the entrance, but his voice was drowned out by the DJ's music.

"What?" Nadia asked, struggling to hear him.

"I said, is it always this loud?" he asked, cupping his mouth with one hand and leaning closer to speak more directly into her ear.

The warmth of his breath on her earlobe created a pleasant sensation that momentarily distracted her. "Pretty much. You'll get used to it, though, and it'll make it easier to stay on the beat when you're dancing."

"If you say so." He smiled wryly as if he didn't believe anything could help him that much and turned fascinated eyes on the dancers who were already on the floor.

"So you'll at least try it?"

"That depends. Do they serve alcohol here?"

"Yes."

"Then maybe."

She laughed. "Come on, let's find a spot to stash our coats." Leading the way around the outskirts of the dance space and waving to a few familiar faces, Nadia wound her way toward an empty seat by the bar.

"Nadia! Over here!"

The sound of her name being called made Nadia look over at a table in the corner where a voluptuous woman with a cloud of blond hair was wiggling her fingers at her to get her attention.

Karen. No, wait…Karina. That was it. A regular on the dance club scene.

"Who's that?" Benji asked from behind her.

"Someone I know from clubbing. We should say hi."

Her gaze landed on another pair of ladies at Karina's table as she led the way over. She knew neither by name, but they looked vaguely familiar. Most likely regulars, too. They nodded at her as she approached, but she didn't miss the way their eyes almost immediately settled on Benji, sizing him up.

Or the unexpected flicker of displeasure she felt at the sight.

Smothering it, she plastered a smile onto her face. "Karina," Nadia greeted the blonde, and the other woman hopped up from the table to give her a quick hug. It wasn't something she normally did, and somehow it seemed as if it was meant more for Benji's benefit than Nadia's, particularly since the hopping motion emphasized Karina's generous assets.

"Sweetie, it's so good to see you! Where have you been hiding yourself lately?" Karina asked, reproach obvious in her tone and her eyes flitting between Benji and Nadia.

"Just been busy with the holidays and everything. You know how it is."

"*Do* I," the other woman returned knowingly as she turned a coy little smile in Benji's direction. "Is this what's been keeping your holidays so busy? Hi, I'm Karina." She offered her hand.

Benji took it.

It was only polite that he do so, but somehow the sight didn't sit well with Nadia. "We were just going to grab a seat at the bar, so…" she started to say.

"The bar? No, sit with us! We'll make room," Karina said, motioning for her two friends to scoot their chairs a little closer together.

"That's really not necessary—"

But Karina had already pulled an unused chair from a neighboring table and added it to theirs. She patted the seat, obviously directing the invitation more towards Benji than Nadia.

Benji only adjusted his glasses and smiled politely before turning to speak to Nadia instead. "Maybe I should get us some drinks first?"

"Perfect," she said, hoping her satisfaction didn't show too much on her face. Margarita?"

"Anyone else?" he asked, ever the gentleman, and there was a chorus of drink orders from the other ladies.

"Coming right up." He disappeared in the direction of the bar, and Nadia—rather reluctantly—draped her coat over a chair and sat down.

Karina leaned in. "He's a cutie pie, Nadia. Is he yours?"

For a split second, Nadia wasn't sure how she wanted to answer that. It was silly, because the whole purpose of taking Benji out dancing was to provide him with a new venue for meeting women. "No, he's just a friend," she said finally. "We're here tonight so I can give him a salsa lesson. He's never danced before."

All three women at the table perked up as if she'd just announced the sale of the century. "Well, we'll be happy to help him practice, won't we, ladies?" Then Karina frowned and gestured at the dance floor. "There are, like, three women for every guy tonight. You were smart to bring your own."

Funny, but Nadia was beginning to question the brilliance of her idea to bring Benji here tonight.

He reappeared behind her then, unfortunately without the drink that Nadia suddenly felt she could really use right about now. "They're going to bring the drinks over," he said as he set his coat down, and then before he could sit, Karina sprang up and wrapped her arm around his as she smiled up at him.

"So I hear this is your first time salsa dancing," she all but cooed. "This is going to be fun."

He blinked. "Oh. Yes, well, let's hope so."

Karina opened her mouth to say something else, and instinct told Nadia that it was going to be an invitation to dance. It was a perfectly normal thing for her to say, especially after Nadia had already told her that she and Benji were merely friends—

—and yet Nadia found herself standing up and stepping in between them to wrap the fingers of her hand around Benji's, breaking the contact between Karina and him. "Yes, it is going to be fun," she agreed with a smile that she hoped looked perfectly pleasant. "Would you excuse us, Karina?"

"Huh? Oh, sure, of course." The blonde's smile faltered momentarily, but she quickly restored it as she took a step back. "But save me a dance!"

Benji's fingers curled around Nadia's in return as she started to pull him toward the crowded dance floor, a perfectly innocent form of contact of which Nadia was far more aware than she had reason to be.

It was the lights, she told herself, and the effect of the music, or maybe it was the drinks making her lightheaded. Then she realized she hadn't had any yet.

"She seems…friendly," Benji said, hard to hear over the music, and all Nadia could seem to do was nod wordlessly in reply and try to ignore the way his comment left a sour taste in her mouth.

Turning to face him on the dance floor, she felt a moment's hesitation before stepping closer to him in the natural dance embrace, which was ridiculous since she had danced like this with countless other men before. If anything, it was far less intimate than the dance frames of most of the other dancers on the floor, and yet she was acutely aware of the warmth his body radiated this close to hers.

Nadia forced her attention onto the dance. "Now," she told Benji, her face inches from his and her eyes locked onto his vivid blue ones, "you put your other arm around me and remember to keep a little tension in both arms, okay?"

He nodded silently, his eyes never leaving her face, and then he slid his free arm very carefully around her waist as if concerned about pulling her too close. His hesitation made her forget her own, and she squeezed his fingers in hers where they joined hands before pulling him just a little bit closer.

"Just follow my lead," she told him, curiously breathless. "And hold on tight."

Then she let the music take over.

❖ Chapter Eight ❖

"YOU'RE DOING GREAT," NADIA encouraged him sometime later, laughing and with any awkwardness forgotten while they danced. "Really, you've got the basic step, you're keeping good time with the music—"

Benji wore a frown of concentration, but at her words, his lips momentarily twitched as if he wanted to smile but couldn't coordinate both smiling and dancing at the same time. "Thanks."

"But you should try not to look at your feet all the time."

"Okay." He raised his head obediently and then two seconds later sent a furtive glance downward.

She grinned at him, feeling a wave of affection. "Fun, huh?"

"You tell me," he said. "You're the one whose feet I've stepped on twenty times."

"Happens to everybody when they first learn. Don't worry about it. Hey, if you're up for it, why don't we try an underarm turn next?"

"Sure."

"And maybe a little hip action."

"Absolutely not."

Nadia did a double take. "What? Why?"

"I'll stick to the footwork and leave the hip action to you."

"But it's salsa," she said reasonably. "You're supposed to move your hips."

"But you see, when *you* move your hips like that, you look good. If *I* try to do it, I'll just look like my underwear's creeping up on me."

A startled laugh escaped her. "I beg your pardon?"

"Hey, you got me on the dance floor. I'd call that a major win for you. Save the rest for another day."

The song came to an end and faded into another, slower number that was better suited to a rhumba than a salsa, or even to the ever-popular seventh-grade slow dance style that was more commonly seen on the dance floor.

After a moment's hesitation, Benji drew Nadia in closer. She let him, although she couldn't seem to look him in the eye and averted her gaze to look over his shoulder instead. It was still a casual dance frame, but she felt a subtle change as they settled into it that was less a shift in style and more a shift in mood.

Her free hand slid very naturally up higher on his arm until it came to rest behind his neck, almost of its own accord, and she felt his hand tighten on her waist in response. It felt good to have it there—maybe too good—and she felt an inexplicable urge to bolt.

What on earth was wrong with her?

"Nadia," he started to say, his voice low and his mouth close to her ear, and her strange need to flee increased.

"You know what?" she interrupted a little too brightly as she pulled back from him, her heart thumping unusually fast. "I'm not really a slow dance kind of girl. Besides, my feet could use a break. Why don't you ask Karina to dance instead? She's been eyeing us this whole time, and I think she's dying to get out on the dance floor with you."

"Oh." Confusion flickered through his eyes. She felt a pang of guilt for having put it there, but her rising anxiety—peculiar as it was—overruled it.

"It's a share-the-wealth kind of thing," she told him, aware that she wasn't really being honest about her reasons but with the words still tumbling from her mouth. "There are so few guys to go around here that it wouldn't be fair to keep you all to myself. Besides, you play your cards right, and you could walk out of here with Karina's number. That's the kind of thing we came here for, right?"

Benji didn't answer her right away. After a moment, he shrugged, his expression unreadable. "If that's what you think is best."

She wasn't so sure that she did, but she turned anyway to gesture for Karina only to discover that the blonde had already appeared right behind her.

"Taking a break?" she said to Nadia while smiling at Benji. "I'd love to take him for a spin."

I'll bet you would, Nadia thought, and then immediately wondered again what was wrong with her. Was that jealousy? That was ridiculous, especially considering how eager she'd been a moment ago to put some distance between herself and Benji—literally. "Absolutely," she said, taking a step back to clear a path for Karina. "He's all yours. Have fun."

And then she gave Benji a quick smile before turning away to leave the dance floor behind her, resisting the urge to look back because she realized she didn't really care to watch Karina wrap her arms around him.

Her margarita had been delivered to the table at some point while she was on the dance floor, and she drank down half of it before realizing what she was doing. Karina's two friends stared at her. "Thirsty," she lied curtly, and one of them nodded politely.

Abandoning the drink, Nadia turned around again to watch the dancers on the floor, her eyes repeatedly drawn back to Benji and Karina. They looked good together, and while Benji moved a trifle stiffly, Karina didn't seem to mind in the least. No, the blonde looked very happy, and—

Oh, come on, woman. Play a *little* hard to get, Nadia thought irritably as Karina pressed herself even closer to Benji.

"Hey there, gorgeous."

Startled by the new voice, Nadia turned her head to see the speaker and recognized the personal trainer who had given her his number last week. Tall, broad-shouldered, and with gleaming white teeth that probably cost him a small fortune, he grinned down at her with his arms folded across his chest in such a way as to emphasize his melon-sized biceps. "Oh," she said, struggling to remember his name. It began with a D, didn't it? "Hi... Dan, right?"

He frowned and even looked taken aback that she might have forgotten him. "Dane."

"Right, sorry," Nadia said, flashing him a quick smile more out of habit than anything else. "Nice to see you." She glanced just as quickly away again as the music switched back to a livelier salsa tune. Her eyes found their way back to the dance floor and Benji just in time to see him flash Karina a half-smile. A response to a joke—or was he flirting?

And why did she care?

Before Nadia could examine her dismay too closely, Dane leaned in a little nearer in a way that gave Nadia no polite choice except to look at him. "So," he continued, smiling once more in a way that Nadia had to admit was rather dazzling, "did you lose my number or something?"

Not consciously, she hadn't, but she couldn't honestly remember where she'd put it now. "Busy week. You know how the holidays get," she returned, finding it harder than usual to muster anything remotely resembling vivaciousness. He was standing a little close for her liking actually, which made no sense to her since she was sure he'd stood every bit as close to her last week when she'd met him, and it had merely seemed like a natural part of their flirtation then. Tonight it just struck her as presumptuous.

"Yeah, I guess," he agreed, although he didn't look completely satisfied with her answer. "Have to come up for air sometime, though. How's next week looking?"

Next week? That suddenly seemed very far away, and all she could think was that going out next week held very little appeal for her. "Probably pretty busy then, too," she said finally, thinking it the gentlest way to turn him down.

He blinked at her in obvious bewilderment, which was no wonder considering the way the women nearest to them were eyeing him with interest. "Oh. Well, how about a dance, then? You've got room in your schedule for that, right?" He grinned again, although this time it seemed slightly forced.

The thought of dancing with him left her lukewarm at best, but after having just shot down his attempt to wrangle a date with her, she supposed a dance would be a harmless enough way to offer an olive branch, socially speaking. Or maybe her conscience was overcompensating after what had happened with Benji a few minutes ago.

In any case, she thought, casting another furtive glance in Benji's direction, a little distraction right now couldn't hurt.

"Sure," she agreed. "Let's dance."

Dane tried to wrap his arm around her waist to lead her out onto the dance floor, but Nadia smoothly slipped free and took his hand instead. As they faced each other, she braced her hand on his shoulder in such a way as to maintain a little space between their torsos, which—judging by the flicker of annoyance in his eyes—had not been part of his original plan.

Plans change, Nadia thought coolly, giving him an even look, and then he gave up and began to lead her in the dance.

Her eyes found Benji by accident, and it might have been her imagination, but he seemed to be relaxing the more he danced with Karina. That was good, Nadia thought, trying to feel sincere and uncomfortably aware that she was failing.

Then Dane turned her, and she lost sight of Benji in the crowd.

Forget everything and just dance already. She forced her attention back to her partner. He was a very attractive man, after all, the kind who caught the eye of every woman he walked past, including—last week—Nadia. He moved well to the music, too, and there was absolutely no reason why she shouldn't enjoy a dance with him. No reason at all.

And yet she wasn't.

Even Dane seemed to realize she was just going through the motions on the dance floor, despite her efforts to make it seem otherwise, because he ratcheted up the moves in which he led her to the point where the couples nearest to them hooted their approval and admiration. And then he turned on the charm. Well, what he seemed to think was charm anyway.

"Baby, the way you move is my every fantasy come true, you know that?" he said, barely audible above the music, and he grinned at her. "And that dress..." He gave a low whistle and shook his free hand as if he'd just singed it on her. "But you'd probably look hot in anything."

The lines he threw at her, all too familiar after years of dating overly confident men like him, seemed suddenly flat to Nadia's ears. Instead of laughing or tossing something similar back as she might normally have done, she found herself wincing inwardly. And for a moment, she wondered if she ought to pretend to twist her ankle just so she could find an excuse to end the dance.

But while she debated whether or not to give in to that urge, Nadia was abruptly caught off guard as Dane managed to circumvent her hold on his shoulder and pull her closer—too close, really.

He leaned in and whispered into her ear, "I bet you'd look hot out of it, too."

Oh, you've got to be kidding me… "You know what?" Nadia said abruptly, tiring of this particular exchange and shoving him a few inches back from her. "I think we're done here. I'm going to sit the rest of this one out."

"What?" Dane protested, laughing. "Come on, loosen up a little."

"You're loose enough for both of us," she returned. "And I'm not interested."

"Not interested?" he repeated, his laughter fading and irritation crossing his face. "What are you talking about? You were plenty interested last week."

"Don't flatter yourself." She turned to leave the dance floor, and Dane caught her by the arm.

"Hey," he said, and his irritation appeared to grow. "You playing games with me or something? Ready to go one minute, turn into an ice princess the next?"

"Take your hand off my arm," she said coolly.

"You aren't seriously walking away from me here? Because I—"

Out of nowhere, Benji's voice interrupted him. "Hey, I think she asked you to let go of her arm."

Both Nadia and Dane did a double take as they turned to see Benji standing behind Dane, a frown on his face and a tautness to his jaw that Nadia would never have believed him capable of producing. His eyes seemed particularly bright as they stared at Dane, bright and unblinking. Karina hovered nervously behind him, the only person to do so, because the nearest dancers moved a wary step or two back as they caught sight of the expression on Dane's face.

Benji surely must have noticed it, too, close as he was to the other man—the other and most definitely *bigger* man. But the only reaction Nadia saw Benji make was a slight twitch to his eyelid.

Dear God, she'd brought him here only to get him killed, Nadia thought, dismayed. Some dating coach she was. She saw Dane's muscles tense, and she hastened to step between the two men. "It's okay, Benji," she told him, putting her hand on his arm. "I'm fine."

"He's bothering you," Benji corrected her, his eyes never leaving Dane.

"I can handle him, believe me."

"Yeah, listen to her, *Benji*," Dane said with obvious disdain, and his expression turned into a leer that he directed at Nadia. "The lady can handle me all she wants."

Oh, please, Nadia thought wearily with an inward eye roll just as Benji frowned more deeply and started to open his mouth again. She tugged on his arm in an attempt to get him to leave the dance floor with her, and he finally turned away from Dane to look at her. "Let it go," she urged. "Let's just go sit down and have a drink."

Benji looked dissatisfied. "But—"

"Hey, Benji?" came Dane's voice, and just as Benji turned his head to look back at the other man, Dane's fist smashed into Benji's face, snapping his head back and sending him staggering back and onto the floor. Dancers gasped and hastily cleared the floor, and when Benji brought his hands away from his face, there was blood streaming from his nose.

Dane smirked down at Benji, who sat up looking more startled than anything else as he wiped blood away. He started to get to his feet.

Dane's smirk grew bigger, and he reformed his fist.

Something inside Nadia snapped, and she was gratified to note that Dane's smug expression disappeared right about the time her fist connected with his jaw.

❖ ❖ ❖

"MORE ICE?" NADIA ASKED Benji as she walked back into her living room with a fresh ice pack.

"Thanks," he said from where he lay on her couch with a half-melted bag of ice on his face. He swapped it for the one she held out to him, and she set the old one in a bowl on her coffee table.

She cringed inwardly at the sight of his swollen nose and cut lip. Considering that his nose seemed to have taken the brunt of the impact, he was lucky it hadn't been broken. His glasses hadn't been quite so lucky, and now they sat on her coffee table with one lens cracked. "How's your nose?"

"Better. How's your hand?"

Nadia flexed her fingers and grimaced, although she couldn't really bring herself to regret taking a swing at Dane. "I'd swear that guy's chin is made of rock."

Benji made a sound that might have been a chuckle, although it came out slightly muffled from underneath the ice pack. "Nice form, by the way. Although I like to think I softened him up for you when I hit his fist with my face."

His words made her smile, but only for a moment, and then she sank down onto the edge of the couch beside him. "Oh, Benji, I'm so sorry. I can't believe this happened."

"You mean you've never punched a guy on the dance floor before?"

"Clubs can get interesting sometimes, but no, that was a first."

"Hey, technically you only said I wouldn't *die* from salsa dancing. I don't believe any such guarantees were made about getting my face tenderized by a seven-foot tall block of granite, so I blame myself."

Nadia was silent, flooded with guilt.

Her silence seemed to alarm him, because Benji quickly removed the ice pack from his face to squint at her with concern. "That was supposed to be a joke, but I guess it was a bad one. Sorry."

"*You're* sorry? You were such a good sport about going tonight, and then you stood up for me with that nimrod and wound up getting flattened for the trouble, and *you're* sorry?"

"Well," he said slowly as he played with the ice pack in his hands, and his lips twitched. "I'm sorry that I didn't duck."

She gave him a look that was tinged with both disbelief and affection, and the affection only grew stronger when the twitch of his lips turned into what could only be described as a cheeky sort of grin.

But then he winced almost immediately. "Ow."

"Your lip is bleeding again. Hang on, I'll get a tissue." Nadia hurried to grab one from the bathroom and returned to sit beside Benji again and dab gently at his injured lip. He grew still and closed his eyes as she did it. "The bruising's going to get worse before it gets better. You're going to look lovely in the morning," she observed after a minute.

"Won't I, though? My co-workers are going to be so impressed. I think I'll tell them I'm in a fight club."

"Think they'll buy it?"

"Maybe not, but it sounds better than 'you should see the other guy after my date beat him up'."

My date. The words jumped out at her. Either Benji didn't realize what he'd said, or he meant the words far more innocently that Nadia generally did. A date could still be perfectly platonic, she supposed, but—

What was she, a sixteen-year-old? She was analyzing his speech like an anxious teenager, searching for clues about his feelings, which—quite frankly—she couldn't remember having done since she really was sixteen.

Then she caught herself noticing the shape of his mouth as she applied gentle pressure to his bleeding lip with the tissue, and she was even more flustered.

The entire evening had left her feeling out of sorts, although maybe part of that was simply a natural result when an evening ended with a fistfight. She felt a pang as she thought of the moment Dane had struck Benji. As mixed-up as she seemed to be at the moment, she was certain of one thing she needed to say.

Benji opened his eyes then, and Nadia took her hand away from his lip.

"Benji," she said softly.

"Yes?"

"What you did tonight, that was very sweet. Thank you."

"Didn't quite have the glorious ending a guy might hope for, but—"

"It was sweet," she repeated.

He was silent.

Nadia started to say something more when she caught sight of the white edge of something poking out at the top of Benji's shirt pocket. "You've got a napkin from the club in your pocket," she said, recognizing the *Luna Bailando* logo on it, and she attempted a joke to lighten the mood. "Commemorative souvenir?"

"Huh? Oh, that." Benji removed it from his pocket and unfolded it. "Your friend Karina stuck that in there right as we were leaving." He examined it with surprise, squinting again. "Looks like her phone number."

Oh. That sour taste from earlier was back in Nadia's mouth.

Pushing himself up into a sitting position, Benji shook his head. "Since when does getting your lights punched out make you more attractive to women?"

"When it happens because you were being gallant," Nadia answered, trying not to sound as dismayed as she suddenly felt. Of course Karina would give him her number; why wouldn't she? And of course Benji would be flattered by it. Maybe even excited.

"If I'd have known that, I'd have tried to get hit in the face sooner." Then Benji touched his nose and winced. "No. No, I probably wouldn't. Never mind."

Crumpling up the bloody tissue in her hand, Nadia stood up. "So, are you going to call her?" She stepped into the kitchen to dispose of the tissue and to hide from Benji what was no doubt a troubled expression on her face.

"Do you think I should?" His voice was unusually quiet.

And suddenly Nadia, who was never at a loss for words, couldn't seem to think of anything to say in response, especially when she felt that odd panic from earlier threatening to return. "Well…"

"Yes?"

"That's the whole reason we went, wasn't it?" she said finally, not quite answering his question. "To help you meet somebody?" Maybe not quite so soon, though, she thought and then berated herself.

"I suppose," he agreed flatly.

"Then I guess that's your answer, isn't it?" she said, returning to the living room and sitting down in a chair instead of on the couch beside him. She smiled a smile that was probably a little too bright and didn't quite look him in the eyes. "Benji Garner. I told you that you were a player."

The corner of his mouth lifted slightly before he winced again, and he folded up the napkin before returning it to his pocket. Then he reached for his fractured glasses and stood up. "I should probably get going."

Nadia rose, too, loathe to discuss Karina anymore but reluctant to see Benji go. "Are you okay to drive? Your glasses—"

"I can still see well enough," he said, peering through them and then putting them on. "Well enough to get me home, at least. Then I'll swap them out for another pair."

"Are you sure?"

Benji nodded and reached for his coat. "Thanks for the ice."

Nadia followed him to the door, absolutely positive she ought to say something more to him but completely at a loss as to what exactly it should be. "I'm sorry about tonight," she said finally, feeling the words inadequate even as she said them.

"Don't be. It was fun up until it turned into an episode of Jerry Springer's show."

This time Nadia's smile was more genuine. "Yes, it was." Then her eyes settled on the edge of the napkin sticking up from Benji's pocket, and her smile faded.

Opening the door to leave, Benji hesitated for a moment, and then he appeared to think better of whatever he was going to say. "Good night," he offered, smiling a half-smile that seemed designed to spare his injured lip any more discomfort.

"Good night," Nadia echoed without her usual energy, and she watched him go with her heart feeling a little heavier than it had before.

❖ Chapter Nine ❖

NADIA HAD THE LATER shift the next day, so when she walked into the bakery, Trish already had the store open for business and was in the middle of explaining to Aimee the difference between delightfully golden brown and just plain burnt.

Putting her purse away and tying on an apron, Nadia stopped directly in front of the other two women.

They both looked up.

"What's wrong with me?" Nadia asked bluntly.

"Oh, so many things," Trish answered cheerfully. "Why?"

"I'm serious, Trish. I think I really screwed up." Nadia slumped back against the kitchen wall. "I thought I was an expert on men and dating. Now I'm not so sure."

"You *are* serious, aren't you? Should we have chocolate on hand for this?"

"Couldn't hurt."

Trish turned to their new hire. "Aimee—"

"I'm on it," the younger woman said, and she disappeared into the front of the bakery only to reappear a minute later with an entire tray of double chocolate fudge brownies from out of the display case.

"That might be overkill," Trish said, looking at Aimee askance.

"Hey, you never know. She looks pretty depressed to me," Aimee returned, setting down the tray and holding out a brownie to Nadia.

"Thanks," said Nadia, and then winced as she took the proffered brownie in her sore hand. She'd iced it again this morning, but it was still hurting. She switched the brownie to her left hand instead.

Trish noticed. "Hey, is it my imagination, or are you babying your right hand?" She bent to get a closer look. "What happened?"

"I punched a guy in the jaw last night."

"You did *what?*" Her friend exclaimed, straightening.

"Did you remember to tuck your thumb?" Aimee asked before Nadia could respond, demonstrating with her own fist. "Like this, see?"

"Not important right now, Aimee," Trish told her, frowning. "Who was the guy? It wasn't Benji, was it?"

"Of course it wasn't Benji. You remember that personal trainer I met last week? Dane? He was at the club last night, and I swear I don't see how his head is big enough to contain his ego. He got a little rude." Jerk, she thought, wishing now that she'd thought to kick him instead, and maybe someplace significantly lower. It would have hurt her a lot less and him a lot more.

"You couldn't have just thrown your drink in his face?"

"He was being a complete tool."

"Yeah, but—"

"And he hit Benji."

Now she had both Trish and Aimee staring at her. She averted her eyes and took a bite of her brownie.

"So you were defending Benji's honor?" Trish said finally.

"More like he was trying to defend mine. Dane just sucker punched him. But that's not why last night got screwed up."

"No?"

Nadia closed her eyes. Her head was beginning to hurt, probably from overthinking things. Either that or from lying awake all night. "I think maybe I might like him."

"Benji?"

A grin of delight spread across Trish's face. "Really?" Then she peered closer, and her smile turned into a frown of confusion. "So why do you look so depressed about it?"

Nadia opened her eyes again to look at Trish, thinking of how she'd pushed Benji toward Karina the night before. "Because the moment I realized it, I tried to do everything I could to encourage him to go out with somebody else."

Both of the other women stared at her like she had sprouted another head. "Kind of an unorthodox method of seduction," Aimee said finally around a mouthful of brownie, her brow furrowing.

"No kidding," Nadia returned tersely. "Who does that?"

"Well—"

"I bolted like he was the big bad wolf and I was the next thing on his menu—at least I tried to. What was I so scared of?" She rubbed her aching head and groaned. "I need caffeine."

"Coming right up," Aimee said, stuffing the rest of her brownie in her mouth and disappearing once more into the front of the bakery.

Nadia looked at her best friend. "Guys don't scare me, Trish. Guys have never scared me. You know that."

"So what's different this time?"

"Benji," Nadia said after a moment, her voice softening as she pictured him. "Benji's what's different."

"Maybe different isn't such a bad thing, though." Trish put her arm around Nadia and gave her a quick and encouraging squeeze. "It's not like other guys you've gotten involved with have ever really rung your bell, have they? From everything you've told me about him, it sounds like Benji might be the kind of guy a girl could really get attached to."

"Yeah, well I don't get attached," Nadia said, and then blinked as the words sank in to her. It was true, she didn't. Not to guys anyway. The guys she went out with were fun, but that was as far as it went. And that had never bothered her, until now. "I don't get attached," she repeated slowly.

Trish studied her thoughtfully. "First time for everything."

"Hey, if you ask me, you are making this way too complicated," Aimee said flatly, reappearing in the open doorway with a steaming cup of coffee in her hand. "If I were you," she continued just as the bell on the door jingled, "I'd just jump the guy and see what happens."

Someone made a coughing sort of sound, and all three women turned to see a wide-eyed and blushing gentleman in a tweed coat peering at them through the open doorway.

"Is…is this a bad time?" he stammered.

You have no idea, Nadia thought.

◆ ◆ ◆

LATER THAT EVENING NADIA curled up on her couch in comfortable PJs with a half-gallon of mint chocolate chip ice cream that she ate right out of the container while she stared at her cell phone. It sat on her coffee table, practically staring right back at her but refusing to ring.

It had been strange to go the entire day without speaking to Benji or seeing him, despite the fact that she'd done so every day of her life up until a few days ago. Somehow, in the short time she'd known him, he'd managed to get under her skin like nobody else, and she couldn't help but wonder if she'd had even remotely the same kind of effect on him.

If she had, though, surely he would have called.

Wouldn't he?

Unless he was as confused as she had been. She'd given him reason to be.

Finally, she reached for the phone. Nadia Normandy was no coward. There was no reason why she shouldn't be the one to make the first move.

Her fingered hovered over the first digit in his phone number.

She might, however, lose just enough nerve to switch to texting instead. *Hey, how's the face?*

There was no immediate reply. Maybe his phone was off. Maybe it was off because he was in the middle of a date. With Karina. Frowning, Nadia began scooping out an enormous bite of ice cream with which to console herself when she saw a response appear on her phone's screen:

Not pretty. How's the hand?

She felt a sliver of relief and texted back. *Sore. Treating it with ice cream now. Sorry about what happened last night.*

Not your fault.

That was debatable. Taking a deep breath, she texted the question that was foremost on her mind. *You call Karina yet?*

A long moment passed before he responded. *No.*

It was amazing how just one little word could make a girl feel so much better. Now what, though?

The topic she most needed to discuss with him was hardly one for the phone.

After another long pause, Benji texted her again. *Better go. Working late.*

An excuse, or the truth? In any case, she reluctantly texted back a polite good night and set the phone back down.

Then she picked up the ice cream again along with her spoon and thoughtfully dug out another bite.

❖ Chapter Ten ❖

NEW YEAR'S EVE. FOR many people it marked the last day of indulgence in sweets before starting a new year and a new diet, and there was a flurry of almost desperate activity in the bakery that day.

"Last minute party treats," one frazzled customer explained to Nadia as she packed up a boxful of assorted delicacies for the woman. "To replace the ones my teenagers got their hands on. Hope they'll go well with champagne."

"Everything goes with champagne," Nadia assured her.

The advantage of such a busy day was that it made the hours fly by very quickly so that closing time came around in what seemed like little more than the blink of an eye. It also made it impossible to spend much time wondering about what a certain accountant was doing.

"No messages?" Trish asked her, seeing Nadia check her phone as they locked the bakery door behind them on their way out.

Nadia shook her head and dropped her phone back in her coat pocket before buttoning her coat closed.

"Maybe he's been too busy working to call."

"Maybe."

Trish wrapped her scarf tightly around her neck and pulled her hat down lower to cover her ears. "You could always call him, you know. It's the twenty-first century. Women woo guys all the time."

"Woo?" Nadia repeated, smiling faintly and raising one eyebrow.

"Yes, woo. It's not a word I get to use often, so cut me some slack. Come on,

Nadia. You're no shrinking violet. Go see the guy. Tell him you like him."

"He might have a hard time believing that after I tried so hard to push him toward Karina."

"So show him that you mean it. Do something special—oh!" Trish's eyes lit up. "Dress up like a million bucks and crash his party tonight! Stuff like that always works great in the movies." She frowned.

"Too bad you don't have any reason to chase after him through an airport. According to modern cinema, that *always* ends well."

"You're a kook, you know."

"Hey, at least consider it. The party crashing, I mean, not the airport. We're about to start a new year here. Why not kick it off with a bang? You don't really want to go to that thing at Marianne's place tonight anyway." She pointed an accusing finger. "You're always giving other people advice on how to handle their personal lives. I think it's high time you let someone else return the favor. Starting with me."

"Mm. I'll see you later," Nadia said, avoiding Trish's question and giving her friend a quick hug. "Enjoy your cookies and milk tonight with Ian and Kelsey, okay?"

Trish grinned. "Do we know how to ring in the New Year, or what?"

"You're a party animal," Nadia said over her shoulder as she turned to go. "Happy New Year, Trish."

"Happy New Year—don't forget to make a resolution," Trish called after her as she left. "Might be a good time to make some changes."

It might. Nadia pulled the collar of her coat up as high as it would go and let her breath out slowly, fogging up the chilly December air as she walked to her car. She stopped beside it and stared thoughtfully ahead of her, not really seeing anything.

Why not go? She was already on her own and missing Benji, so what did she really have to lose besides a little of her dignity? Maybe a grand gesture *would* be appropriate, if crashing a New Year's Eve party of an accounting firm could be called grand. If nothing else, it might show Benji that her feelings for him were most definitely not mixed anymore.

Of course, she realized with dismay as she got into her car and put the key in the ignition, she didn't actually know where Benji's party was being held. That could be a problem.

Unless one knew of a person who kept pretty close tabs on the personal lives of those around her.

Leaving the key unturned, Nadia pulled her phone back out and dialed her newest coworker's number.

"Hello?"

"Hi, Aimee. I need to ask your Gram something…"

◆ ◆ ◆

MACGREADY FINANCIAL SERVICES, INC. must have been doing pretty well for itself, because the business partners had arranged for the company's party to be held in an event room in one of the city's finer hotels. Glitz and glamour were the norm at the Wentworth Grande, and for just a moment, Nadia's confidence wavered as she approached it.

Strains of music greeted her as soon as she stepped into the lobby. A live band, by the sound of it. It was jazzy music, and whoever the lead singer was, her voice was smooth and sultry, like liquid velvet. The tune she sang was vaguely familiar, something from a bygone era that Nadia had probably heard playing in the background of a movie once upon a time. Something by Ella Fitzgerald maybe... It brought to mind images of elegance and class. And romance.

Cheek to Cheek, she thought suddenly, and an image of Ginger Rogers and Fred Astaire danced through her mind, although she had no idea from what movie it might have been.

The lobby's high ceilings were adorned with dangling globes of gold and white in assorted sizes, and for a moment she had the absurd thought that some poor patsy must have had a nightmare of a time hanging those things. They were lovely, though, and when combined with the sparkling streamers that must have been equally difficult to put up, they served to create an atmosphere of extravagant celebration.

All right then, Nadia thought, slipping off her coat to reveal the slim and strappy blue dress underneath it. Good thing she'd dressed for the occasion.

It had been years since she'd crashed a party, mostly because nowadays she usually received invites to all of the good ones anyway, but she still remembered the key to pulling off a party crash successfully.

Confidence.

Few people questioned a woman who breezed into a room as if she belonged there. If she could manage that part well enough, it should be simple enough to mingle inconspicuously until she found Benji. And then—well, and then she was going to have to wing the rest.

Nadia followed the music and proceeded toward the room that housed the party, sidestepping streamers and pausing just long enough to add her coat to the collection of wraps already in the gilded hall. Her nerves fluttered for a moment. It's only Benji, she told herself, but that only made it worse. Telling herself not to be a baby about it, she squared her shoulders and pushed open the grand double doors to enter the room.

Mrs. B had been absolutely correct about the location of the party. What she had either not known about it or failed to pass along to Nadia was the fact that, from the balloons and streamers that were everywhere to the pillars and tabletop centerpieces arranged around the room, there was a black and white theme to the party that became immediately apparent as Nadia stood in the open doorway in her bright and extremely *not* black or white dress.

The properly attired people nearest to her did double takes and stared at the brilliant flash of blue that was Nadia, and she felt her face grow warm.

Ah, and the walls of the room were made up almost entirely of mirrors, too, which meant her bright blue dress was reflected back at her and everyone else at every turn.

Perfect.

Not quite the inconspicuous entrance she was going for. Which meant she probably had about ten seconds to find Benji before someone set security on her. And of course there would be security here tonight. Places like this always had plenty of it on hand. So much for making a grand gesture.

The one advantage to standing out like a sore thumb was that it meant everyone soon noticed her presence as she hovered there in the doorway, and everyone included Benji. She saw him talking with a pair of older gentlemen, a drink in his hand that he was just about to take a sip from when he spotted her. He froze and then slowly lowered the drink, the expression on his face—his poor, *bruised* face after what had happened the other night—turned to one of shock.

Perhaps waiting on his doorstep for him to show up after the party would have been a better idea, Nadia thought belatedly. Chilly, yes, but still grand enough and a lot less likely to get Benji in trouble with his boss. Maybe she ought to turn around and make a run for it before anyone knew she was here to see him.

Before she could do so, he excused himself from his companions and made his way over to her. Rapidly. "Nadia?"

She tried to think of something appropriate to say and came up with very little, acutely aware of the large number of eyes watching them. "I—Hello."

"Why—" His eyes travelled up the full length of her as if they couldn't help themselves. "What are you doing here?"

"Hopefully not getting you fired. I'm so sorry, I thought I'd be able to slip in unnoticed."

He gave her an incredulous look. "Nadia, I doubt you've ever gone anywhere without people noticing you."

His words sent a thrill of pleasure through her. How had she ever thought this man needed help with women?

"Come on," he said, glancing around at their growing audience and lowering his voice. "Let's step out in the hall. Either that or sell tickets." He put his hand on the small of her back—which was bare thanks to her backless dress—and guided her toward the door.

That brief touch was enough to cause a delicious sort of shiver to go up her spine. "I'm sorry," she said again as they emerged into the hallway. They passed a laughing couple just arriving at the party, and Nadia hesitated. This wasn't exactly a conversation for which she wanted an audience. Quite frankly, she wasn't entirely sure she wanted to be present for it herself. "Can we just—" She motioned for Benji to follow her and led the way to a quiet corner.

His eyes were full of questions and no small amount of confusion. Such dazzling blue eyes. They made it difficult to think clearly when he was standing this close to her.

"I'm sorry," she blurted out a third time, thinking now that maybe winging it hadn't been such a brilliant idea after all.

"You said that already. I really don't think you need to worry about it. Other than a sparkling debate about tax codes, you didn't interrupt much."

"I didn't get you in trouble?"

Benji's expression turned incredulous. "You're kidding, right? First this," he said, pointing to the bruises on his face, "which I was very mysterious about, by the way, and then you show up. I'm going to be the coolest guy in the office. Which, granted, may not be saying much."

She winced as she studied the marks on him, her fingers twitching as she resisted the urge to examine them for herself up close and personal. "Does it hurt?"

"Only when I shave. Or chew. Or, you know, breathe."

"I'm—"

"Don't say you're sorry again," he interrupted her, holding up one hand. Despite the guarded look in his eyes, he looked like he might be tempted to smile. But only briefly.

"Okay, I won't."

They stood there in silence for a long moment, and Nadia found herself twisting the tiny strap of her beaded clutch between her fingers. She forced herself to stop, very unfamiliar with this flustered-by-men thing and not caring for it much.

"Nadia?"

"Yes?"

"You didn't actually come all the way down here to check on how my face was doing, did you?"

"I needed to talk to you."

"Tonight?"

"Well, it didn't seem like the kind of thing that should wait until next year," she said with more lightness than she felt. "Nice tux, by the way. You look good." Very good. Any woman in her right mind would love to walk into a party on his arm. A sudden thought occurred to her then, and her mustered lightness dissipated. "Oh. Am I... keeping you from someone? I mean—as in a date?"

A shadow flickered over his expression. "If you're asking if Karina's in there, no, she's not. Look, Nadia, I know she's your friend, and you think I ought to call her up, but the problem is—"

"I don't want you to call her."

He blinked. "You don't?"

She shook her head.

Frowning slightly as if he was having a hard time following her, Benji ran a hand through his hair in a gesture Nadia had long ago come to recognize as restrained frustration. "Then I guess I really do need a dating coach, because I could have sworn that's the message you were sending me."

"About that—" Nadia lowered her eyes to the level of his collar. It was so much easier to think straight when she wasn't looking directly at his face. Although the bit of throat exposed by his collar was surprisingly distracting. "I may not be the expert on men and women that I thought I was, at least not when it comes to myself."

"No?"

"I've had a great time with you this week, Benji. And after a while, I think it seemed a little too great. And I'm not used to that."

Benji grew very still as she spoke.

"And I'm not sure why that made me so jumpy. Maybe it's just how I am, or maybe it's because I watched what I thought was a good thing between my parents fall apart." Or maybe she just needed extensive therapy, she thought, feeling woefully inept as she struggled to explain something she didn't fully understand herself. "Either way, I have a history of not letting men get too close. I've never had any trouble telling a guy goodbye, but it turns out I have a hard time inviting one to stick around. The thing is..."

"Yes?" he prompted her when she trailed off, and he seemed intensely interested in her response.

She made herself look him in the eye again. "You've made me rethink my position on that particular subject."

He stared at her for a minute before speaking. "Your position," he said finally.

"Yes."

"Just to be clear—because I've misinterpreted before—are you talking about your position on me or on men in general?"

"You."

"I see."

His expression was impossible to read, and her pulse sped up a little more as she began to wonder if she'd misread signals from him. "Well—that is, if you're interested in—"

"Nadia?"

She faltered. "Yes?"

He cocked his head at her almost quizzically. "I let you rearrange my closet and take me salsa dancing. Does that tell you anything?"

"Oh," she said, feeling noticeably better. "Well, I told you I wasn't such an expert on the opposite sex after all."

"I don't know about that." Benji cleared his throat. "I think you might be selling yourself a little short. You're still my go-to source for dating expertise. In fact, I could really use some guidance in a very particular social matter."

"I beg your pardon?" Nadia blinked, taken aback by his request. "You want dating advice? Now?"

"Absolutely now." He shoved his hands into his pants pockets and leaned casually back against one wall, his eyes never leaving her. "Hypothetically speaking, suppose a guy happened to be crazy about a particular woman, but it turns out she's a little on the skittish side, and he doesn't want to scare her off—"

"Skittish?"

"Yes." He gave her a pointed look before continuing. "Say this guy finally gets this woman alone outside a party—"

"This woman he's crazy about? Just so we're clear."

"Yes, her. Say he's thinking this might be an exceptionally good time to kiss this woman, which he's wanted to do since he first met her, actually. What would be the best way for this man to go about achieving the desired result in this situation? In your expert opinion."

"Hypothetically speaking?"

"Hypothetically speaking, yes."

"Well," Nadia suggested, leaning back against the wall across from him and feeling her pulse speed up. "I'd recommend he be very direct."

"Direct," Benji repeated, straightening and crossing the short distance between them slowly and very deliberately. He stopped right in front of her. "Got it."

"But no sudden movements, you know. If she's skittish. No woman likes to be lunged at."

"Take it slow, then?" he asked, resting one hand on the wall behind her and looking into her eyes from mere inches away.

"For starters," she said. The things he was doing to her insides with just a look…

"And how will he know when to make his move?"

"Oh, she'll let him know."

"Really? How will she do—"

Nadia cut him off with a kiss, curling her fingers into his hair and pulling him close as he wrapped his arms around her in return. Strong lips, she thought, feeling increasingly lightheaded. Very strong lips. Benji Garner was just full of all sorts of wonderful surprises.

"Do all accountants kiss like this?" she said against his mouth finally, hearing the breathlessness in her voice and delighted by it.

"I don't know," he murmured back. "I haven't kissed any. But if you're really curious to find out, there's a whole roomful of them over there."

She started to laugh, and then he found her lips again and laughter was forgotten.

They might have remained that way indefinitely, but a few minutes later someone cleared his throat, and Benji and Nadia broke apart to see a white-haired gentleman in a terribly expensive suit eyeing them from the doorway he was just about to enter to get to the party.

"Mr. MacGready," Benji greeted him quickly, sputtering slightly and turning red. "Great party, sir."

"Apparently so," the older man returned, and despite his dour demeanor, there was a twinkle in his eye. "You do realize it won't be midnight for another two hours, don't you, Mr. Garner?"

Nadia wrapped her arms around Benji's neck again and grinned at the older man. "We're practicing."

"I see. Carry on, then." And the man disappeared back into the party with the sound of chuckling.

Benji made a choking sound and sighed.

"Your boss?" Nadia asked him.

"Yes."

"He likes me."

"So do I," said Benji, turning his attention back to her. "Where were we again?"

Nadia showed him.

❖ Epilogue ❖

"CAREFUL, YOU DON'T WANT to overmix the dough," Nadia cautioned Benji, retrieving a pair of cookie sheets from one of her kitchen cupboards and then returning to his side. "Just gently fold in the chocolate chips. Like this, see?"

She took the large wooden spoon from him and slipped in between him and the mixing bowl to demonstrate. It was a move that left Benji in a perfect position for wrapping his arms around Nadia's waist, which he immediately did. He also brushed her hair aside so he could trail his lips down the side of her neck.

"You're not paying attention," Nadia said, not really minding at all.

He continued on with what he was doing. "Sorry. Much more pressing matters to deal with here."

"Hey, you're the one who thought it would be nice to give Mrs. B cookies as a thank-you for her meddling. Shouldn't you be participating a little?"

"I intend to participate a lot."

Nadia turned around. "I meant with the baking."

"Oh."

She slid her arms around his neck. "Did you ever have any intention of making cookies with me today, or was it all just a ruse to get into my apartment and practice the art of seduction, cookie-style?"

Benji sighed and hung his head. "She's on to me."

"Not yet, I'm not, honey." She gave him a sly sideways glance. "But if you play your cards right, I might be."

He blinked, and then they both forgot the cookies for a moment when she kissed him again, and he pressed her up against the refrigerator.

A few minutes later, they came up for air, and Nadia remembered the bowl of dough sitting out on the counter. "There are raw eggs in that dough."

He nodded and kissed her again.

"If we're going to get those cookies in the oven," she said against his mouth, "we should probably do it soon—"

"Uh huh," he agreed, not pausing for a moment in what he was doing.

And a few more minutes later, Nadia said, "You know, she likes flowers, too. Maybe we should just send her some flowers."

"Flowers it is," said Benji, and then Nadia started to laugh as they slowly slid down the refrigerator door and to the floor...

The End

Author's Note

Thank you for reading <u>Love Lessons</u>! I hope you enjoyed the story. Now that you've read it, I hope you'll consider leaving a review because reviews are a great way for readers to discover new books. I would sincerely appreciate it!

About the Author

Christine S. Feldman writes both novels and feature-length screenplays, and she has placed in screenwriting competitions on both coasts. She lives in the Pacific Northwest with her ballroom-dancing husband and their beagle. Visit her on Facebook at https://www.facebook.com/ChristineSFeldman or follow her on Twitter at https://twitter.com/FeldmanCS.

Discover other titles from Christine S. Feldman:

Coming Home

The Bargain

Heavenly Bites Novella #1: Pastels and Jingle Bells

Heavenly Bites Novella #2: Love Lessons

Heavenly Bites Novella #3: Playing Cupid

All's Fair in Love and Weddings

Winging It

The Encore

It Happened One Night (Adventures in Blind Dating #1)

Center Stage (Adventures in Blind Dating #2)

The Fix-Up Mix-Up (Adventures in Blind Dating #3)

Made in the USA
Monee, IL
13 April 2023

31774269R00085